D0387550

A
MANSION
AND ITS
MURDER

A MANSION AND ITS MURDER

BY
Robert Barnard
WRITING AS
Bernard Bastable

Carroll & Graf Publishers, Inc.
New York

First Carroll & Graf edition 1998

Carroll & Graf Publishers, Inc.
19 West 21st Street
New York, NY 10010

Library of Congress Cataloging-in-Publication data is available
ISBN: 0-7867-0515-9

Manufactured in the United States of America

FOR
DUDLEY GREEN
WITH FRIENDSHIP AND RESPECT

A
MANSION
AND ITS
MURDER

CHAPTER ONE

Fateful Evening

My earliest memory is of Mr. Gladstone. His face has still a vivid presence in my mind: whiskery, the flesh sagging, the skin discolored, resembling a thin, decaying sort of parchment. Above all, I remember the eyes, which contrived to be both bleared and sharp at the same time. He looked down at me and I sensed—or persuaded myself—that he was actually interested in me. Even today, fifty years after his death, I hope that I was not deceived by the simulated interest in people that is a politician's stock-in-trade.

No, I do not believe it was that. Little girls are sharp, and I was exceptionally sharp for my age.

I expect I remember Mr. Gladstone rather than any other old gentleman who dined with us—and there were many, many who did—because of the excessive flurry, almost amounting to panic, that had all day taken grip of the house. My nanny at the time was one of a long succession of nannies who by then was beginning to take her approaching departure for granted. I had told my father whenever I saw him (which was not often) that I needed to be *taught* things, needed a governess (girls in my family did not go away to school). Meanwhile, my regime was one of benign (or, in the case of my mother, not particularly benign) neglect. The part of the house I haunted was below stairs, the only place where I was something of a favorite. It was below stairs where the flurry was particularly intense. The vast kitchens and the "usual offices" were in a condition of stately hysteria.

"Mr. Gladstone is a great man," said Mr. McKay, the butler, in response to my question as to who the important guest was. He regarded that as all the answer that needed be, so I had perforce to be content with it.

The hysteria was most intense around the great ovens where the meal was being prepared—everything from the splendid salmon, the pheasants, the sirloin of beef, through the aromatic sauces prepared by our French chef (who unlike most French chefs actually came from France) down to the little almond cakes that Mr. Gladstone was said particularly to like, one batch of which went slightly wrong, to my great profit and delight.

"No more of them," said Mrs. Needham, vast and imposing, but kindly behind the facade. "We can't have you being sick if we're going to give you a peek, can we?"

The "peek" was the great treat I was looking forward to, without quite understanding why.

There can be few elderly women in this year of 1946 whose first memories are of Mr. Gladstone, and I should explain that we were not in fact one of the great Liberal families who might have been expected to entertain him from time to time. In fact, he was staying in the area with one such family, the Mastertons of Hazelhurst Manor, and he would be arriving in the family carriage with Lord Masterton (there was no Lady Masterton—she had died many years before, in childbirth). It would not be true to say that we were, in modern parlance, politically uncommitted, but we were not party political. We would have entertained the Marquis of Salisbury with the same degree of pomp as we displayed for Mr. Gladstone—but with less nervousness, for no one thought the Tory leader a Great Man, as the People's William undoubtedly was. More, he was a living legend.

We were impartial politically because we were bankers: Fearing's Bank was one of the great financial institutions which had made the

City of London the center of the world's business. We retained excellent relations with the leading men of both political parties. We would have lavishly feasted Beelzebub if he had happened to be either Prime Minister or Leader of the Opposition.

Much of what I think I remember about that day were things that were told to me later, I expect. Mr. McKay and Mrs. Needham were fixtures at Blakemere for many years after that year of 1884, and they talked of Mr. Gladstone's dinner often—it was a sort of landmark day. In fact, Blakemere, though an immense and drafty pile of echoing corridors, distant ceilings, and excessively heavy decoration, did somehow manage to retain the loyalty of its vast army of domestics, and many of the people who were rushing around frantically below stairs that day remained there until they retired or died, and were friends to me in my young womanhood and later—companionable fixtures in a changing world. Certainly I saw few other people that day in the hours leading up to dinner: my mother was occupied with dressing herself (drearily, I have no doubt), and my father was demonstrating his independence by taking a couple of guests out shooting. My nanny was probably penning letters of application for similar positions. So I was below stairs during the presentation of other guests to the Great Man, and the mixing and mingling that preceded eating, below stairs when the guests were paired off, strictly in accordance with rank and political or local importance, and below stairs when the great silver tureens of turtle soup were taken up to commence the grand dinner.

It was, I suppose, around eight o'clock when, on a signal from one of the footmen racing between the dining hall and kitchens, Beatrice came and put out her hand. I took hers willingly. It was the hand of all others that I was most familiar with. She was the closest thing to a mother I had for many years, until she left Blakemere for unhappy marriage and very happy motherhood. Together we toiled up the stone steps, into the main house (that word is ridiculously inadequate), then down the endless corridors of which I saw little higher than the skirting boards, until finally we came to one of the doors to the Great Hall. Beatrice had chosen the door carefully, to give me the best possible view of our distinguished guest. She opened it a crack, then slipped me just inside it.

"Keep very quiet," she admonished. "Don't do any of your sillies to get noticed."

Ha! It was precious little I was noticed in that house, sillies or no sillies.

I stood there, tiny and wide-eyed. It was not just I who was dwarfed, but everyone at table, everyone in the room. Even the great Mr. McKay seemed merely a fraction of his normal self. The Great Hall was inspired by—no, modeled on—a medieval banqueting hall, as envisaged by one of the illustrators of Sir Walter Scott. It rose up still higher than most of Blakemere's ground-floor rooms, leaving nothing above it but servants' bedrooms, and its ceiling was raftered with great oak beams. Lower down, the nineteenth-century predominated. The long table supported like a circus strongman an endless series of tureens, sauce boats, roasting platters, épergnes, and brilliant crystal glasses and decanters. Footmen were everywhere filling glasses, whipping away plates and serving dishes as one course succeeded another, and I stood there feeling more than ever a nothing amid this endless bustle of magnificence. As a relief from it I raised my eyes to the ceiling—miles it seemed, above me—but the great beams were so distant. And when I lowered my eyes from them, clutching Bea's hand still more tightly, I really saw for the first time Mr. Gladstone.

He was seated to the right of my grandpapa, and he was talking in a gracious, measured manner, listening now and then, and then talking again in what was virtually a monologue with interludes. I had never found my grandfather's conversation interesting, so I understood why our honored guest preferred to do the the talking himself. No one else in his vicinity, not even my uncle Frank, seemed courageous enough to take part in the conversation. It was at some point in this stately duologue, following an interjection from my grandfather, Sir Joseph Fearing, that our distinguished guest took up his glass and, before replying, looked speculatively around.

And saw me, standing diminutive in the doorway by Beatrice's side. He considered for a moment. Perhaps my grandfather's remark had been difficult to reply to; perhaps it had been beneath his notice. After a moment he put down his glass, meditated, and after a glance at my grandfather, beckoned me.

Horror of horrors! I shrank back. Bea, who was one of the senior parlormaids, knew there could be only one response. Grasping my little paw still more firmly, she advanced, curtseyed to Grandpapa as she skirted the head of the table, then arrived by the seat of the Great Man, placed me within his view, then curtseyed and withdrew a pace.

I curtseyed, too. I had been well brought up by the servants.

"Well, young lady, and what is your name?"

He seemed immensely grand. Too grand to talk to a little girl at all. But also whiskery, dry of skin, watery of eye.

"Sarah Jane Fearing," I said, my voice shaking.

He nodded gravely. "And how old are you, Sarah Jane Fearing?"

"Five years and seven months."

"So you've come to watch us feasting, have you?" he asked, his face crumbling into a smile. "What do you think of it, eh?"

I considered.

"I've never seen so much food," I said.

"And none of it for you!" he said roguishly. "That doesn't seem fair, does it?"

I shook my head vigorously.

"But we can soon remedy the situation," he assured me. "What would you say to one of these fine juicy apricots?"

I considered again. I thought he approved of that.

"I should prefer, if you please, sir, three of those little almond cakes."

The reply seemed to delight him. The bags on his face began to bob up and down, and his old eyes lost their film and seemed to sparkle as he looked first at my grandfather and then at my dear uncle Frank who was sitting opposite.

"Now why, Sarah Jane Fearing, do you specify *three* of the little almond cakes?"

"Because the cakes are very small and the apricots are a good size," I replied, gaining confidence.

That delighted him still more.

"A very good answer! The girl is a mathematician. She should be a credit to Fearing's Bank when she grows up. The future is with the ladies, you know."

And he counted out, one by one, three of the little almond cakes from one old hand to the other, put them into my outstretched mitt with another crumbly smile, then turned back to the company with a gesture of dismissal. Beatrice curtseyed, I curtseyed, and we made our way quietly and swiftly out of the Hall.

As I sit here writing and thinking in the tiny parlor of the gatehouse, looking over the mile and a half of intervening grounds to where Blakemere rears its ridiculous bulk in the distance, I remember those two minutes that sealed my destiny as vividly as if it were yesterday.

Sealed my destiny. An absurd phrase? Ridiculous? The foolish jumping to conclusions of the childish mind? I used to think so. But when in 1934 I decided to open Blakemere to the public on Saturdays and Sundays in the summer months, I had the librarian prepare a little leaflet about the house and its history. Even in a long line of splendid entertainments for people of importance, the grand dinner for Mr. Gladstone warranted a mention. He had been feasted at Blakemere on September the tenth, 1884. The new will made by my grandfather which left the house, bank, and practically everything else to his elder son Claudius and his heirs male, failing that to his son Francis and his heirs male, and failing that to the female heirs of his elder son, was made, signed, and witnessed on September the twenty-first of the same year.

The document that sealed my fate.

Last Saturday, having begged a couple of gallons of petrol, I took the two dogs over to Wybush Common. A ridiculous waste, you might say, in a time of great scarcity of petrol and of everything else: the dogs have mile upon mile of the Blakemere estates to run around in.

But dogs like change as much as humans do. I sometimes get as oppressed by the vastness of the grounds around the great house as I used to get by the vastness of the interior of the place when I lived in it. The dogs appreciated the gesture: they ran around in delighted surprise when I let them out of the car, and Lizzie straightaway went and did her business in the little front garden of a cottage on the Common's edge.

"Here, look what your filthy bitch has done!" came a strident voice.

I groaned internally. One of those. I felt like shouting, in the words of Tess of the D'Urberville's mother, " 'Tis nater, and what do please God!" Instead, I just whistled the animals and set off toward the Common. But a hard-faced harridan had appeared at the little wicket gate.

"It's people like you that give dog-owners a bad name!" she shrieked.

I turned.

"It's people like you give people a bad name," I bellowed.

I set off again, rather pleased with myself. Worsting a fishwife shouldn't have given me satisfaction, but it did. When I analyzed my feelings, I realized it was because we had traded insults on a level footing. She had not had the faintest idea who I was. Twenty years ago, I would have been known by everybody here—by everybody within a much wider radius of Blakemere. Fifty years ago, they would have known the whole family—my grandparents, my parents, my uncle Francis, my spinster aunts, even my aunt Clare who had married beneath her and moved away.

Now I could be shouted at by a shrew who had not a notion who I was. And perhaps she would have shouted even if she had known. The war has changed everything. Firmly rooted families have moved away, the men to join up, the women to work in munitions factories and food factories. War widows and solitary service wives have moved into cottages to take advantage of the cheapness of the country. They have no knowledge of the customs and traditions of the place, nor of the great families who ruled the area by virtue of offering opportunities of employment.

As I turned at the brow of Wybush Common, I saw the woman, hovering near her gate, waiting for a second round. I reflected that if she had a husband who had come through the war, he would do well to refuse to be demobbed.

But I am light of heart. Where once Blakemere was known throughout Buckinghamshire, now we—I—am nothing.

That suits me very well. I have had a lifetime of my family. I have made something of my life, but it has been, until the last few years, in their sphere, on their terms, lumbered with their appalling mansion. I have had more than enough of my family. Of its magnificence. Of its guilt.

CHAPTER TWO

Get Thee a Wife

When I was alone during my childhood, which did not happen as often as you might imagine, I would often take myself off to some distant paved space of which the architect of our monumental pile had provided plenty, and play skipping games based on the names of my three aunts.

Sarah, Clare and Jane,
Jane is rather plain

I would chant, or rather mutter under my breath.

Jane and Clare and
Sarah,
Sarah's slightly fairer.

But only slightly, I said to myself.

Sarah, Jane and Clare,
Clare is never there.

Here was what I meant, but here didn't rhyme with Clare. Sometimes when the aunts had annoyed me, my rhymes about them would get nastier, such as "Jane gives me a pain" or "Sarah's slightly squarer" or "Clare is hard to bear."

This may give the impression that my father's sisters loomed much larger in my young life than they actually did. Jane lived at Blakemere, was indeed plain, but was not the acidulated spinster of popular mythology. She was busy, charitable, and advised me constantly on my behavior, probably because no one else did. Sarah had fled the outsize nest and lived in an old farmhouse with a large garden near Wentwood, leasing out the fields and grazing pastures to other farmers in the area. She would have been called a bluestocking in an earlier age. She dabbled in botany, professed atheism, and always gave me excellent teas if I called on a visit. Clare had married beneath her—an artist of all things—and had gone to live in a part of London that was not even Chelsea. She was sometimes invited back to be pitied.

I think my aunts loomed larger in my childhood imagination than in its actuality because of what they represented: possibilities for myself when I grew up, something I began to think about in the years after Mr. Gladstone's momentous visit. I rejected the possibility represented by my aunt Jane, but neither of the other two destinies seemed particularly attractive either. Being a romantic, reading sort of child, I did not rule out the possibility of someone incredibly handsome of my own class (whatever that was—could you have landed bankers?) falling desperately in love with me, and our living happily ever after somewhere not too close to Blakemere. I did not even rule out the possibility of my being carried off by a dusky North African in white robes. On the other hand, I didn't count on it.

The children I could most often find to play with in the intervals between lessons (the intervals were as long and frequent as the lessons, for my governesses were in the early days as ill chosen and ill supervised as my nannies had been) were generally the offspring of servants, gardeners, or higher employees of the family (secretaries, librarians, managers, and so on). Once they got over any awe they might feel at playing with the daughter of the house, they tended rather to pity me.

"Don't you *ever* see your mummy and daddy?" they would ask.

"Of *course* I do," I would reply stoutly, since it seemed to be the sort of thing to do, to have contact with your mother and father. When I grew slightly older my reply changed to: "*Quite* as much as I want to."

My father, Claudius Meyer Fearing, was in his own estimation caught in a cleft stick: he was neither banker nor country gentleman. Others felt he had constructed the cleft stick himself: he was unhappy at the Bank because he was not in overall charge, and he was unhappy at Blakemere for the same reason. He seemed temperamentally unable to subject himself to the rigorous preparation necessary to be a successful banker, and he mostly occupied himself with the pleasanter side of a country gentleman's life—shooting, fishing, and agricultural events (he never completely mastered horsemanship, so he didn't hunt). He was, at that time, something of a congenital malcontent, and one who could give himself wholeheartedly to nothing. When he saw me he was kind to me, inquired about my lessons, occasionally even played with me. If I was not in front of his eyes I was not in his mind. Even when he encountered me unexpectedly in the high, wide corridors of Blakemere he seemed to have to remind himself who I was.

My mother had been married to provide an heir for Blakemere. She had, with some difficulty, produced me, and had then been told that she could have no more children. She had retreated into self-regard and self-pity (and self- a lot of other things as well), gradually making a sort of prison for herself—none the less a prison for being luxurious and undemanding. I could be as high-spirited, adventurous, demanding, or masterful as I wanted, but that would cut no ice with my mother. They were qualities admired in men, but they did not alter the fact that I was not, and could never be, a boy.

"We have to think of the future."

I heard the words, spoken in my grandfather's measured, I would now say pompous tones, through a partially opened window in the library. I had retreated alone, to the little square courtyard just beside it, where I had marked out a hopping game. The library had a long, windowless wall just beside the courtyard, so if hopping palled I could play ball against it. When I heard the words I paused, then peeped round the corner, and edged along to where the window was. I stood beside it and peeked cautiously in. The bookcases in the library rose to the ceiling, and were filled with unread, unreadable leather tomes. It was only much later I realized that many of the books were literally unreadable: the upper shelves were mere painted books, in the trompe l'oeil manner. I was very surprised by this because I had never imagined my grandfather, then well dead, had a sense of humor.

Along the long library table the family was ranged: Grandpapa, Grandmama, my father, my mother (wonder of wonders!), Aunt Jane, Aunt Sarah, my grandfather's private secretary, Cousin Anselm who was a Father of Sons, and therefore of importance to the family firm, and my dear, dear uncle Francis—Uncle Frank, I always called him.

Who was tipping himself backward in his chair, smiling, and stroking his lovely fair beard—short and rather sporty—his eye glinting as he smiled with the utmost complacency at the family Inquisition.

"I've always rather gone for the idea of 'Sufficient unto the day is the evil thereof,' " he said. Retribution was immediate and, for him, probably very satisfying.

"Since you were a boy," thundered my grandpapa, "you have twisted the Scriptures for your own selfish ends."

"Twisted?" said Uncle Frank, unperturbed. "I should have thought 'Take no thought for the morrow' was pretty clear and explicit. It is a great satisfaction to me to be able to say that I never do."

"To call the Bank 'evil' that has made the family fortunes—and that means *your* fortunes—is unforgivable. It is rank ingratitude."

Uncle Frank's lovely fair eyebrows raised themselves satirically.

"Nevertheless for me it *is* an evil, and I see no reason why I should regulate my conduct by any concern for its future."

My grandmother leaned forward. She was by birth a Meyer, one of a prominent converted Jewish banking family. Her lean face was handsome still, her eyes alight with intelligence. She was, I am sure, much cleverer than my grandfather, though she constrained herself within the usual boundaries laid down for married women at the time.

"Fearing's Bank is one of the great financial institutions of this country," she said emphatically. "On it thousands of lives and livelihoods depend. It is time you faced up to your responsibilities, Francis. You have had time enough to sow your wild oats."

"The trouble is, I seem to have more wild oats than most to sow," smiled Frank.

"Marriage will cure that."

Uncle Frank laughed out loud. "That's what I'm afraid of. And to what end? Claud and Harriet have a daughter." (Here my mother sobbed.) "If you insist on sons, Clare and Alfred—at long last—have two, or is it three? There are"—here he nodded in the direction of Anselm Fearing—"cousins. Not cousins galore, but cousins enough. Why should I be the sacrificial lamb?"

"Because if you do not do as we insist, your debts will not be paid," said my grandfather fiercely. Uncle Frank gave a little chuckle. I had the feeling that this threat was not unexpected—was a traditional move in the family chess game.

"That will look good in the newspapers, won't it?" Uncle Frank said mockingly. " 'Banker's son arrested for debt.' 'Bankruptcy proceedings against Fearing's Bank scion.' Well, at least it would rid you of a modicum of your stuffiness."

His mother leaned forward.

"You are forgetting, Francis, that there will come a time when we shall be forced to choose between paying your bills and letting you be disgraced publicly, and the latter will be the less painful alternative."

"But that time has hardly been reached yet, Mama," said Frank. I snatched another look: he was still wonderfully relaxed and genial—a soft toy surrounded by rigid dolls. "My debts, on the scale of younger son's debts in general, are fairly modest: a European tour when one reaches one's majority is traditional, though my tour had its untraditional side; my expeditions have mostly been small in scale and have benefited human knowledge; my London flat is hardly expensive in the family's scale of expenditure. How can you sit in"—he waved his hand around—"*this place* and talk about having to choose whether to pay a few quite reasonable bills for me?"

"It's not just a question of debts," said my grandfather. "*Two* children in the county—"

"Wild oats. And like the gentlemen we aim to be I chose not to dispute the paternity."

"Scandals of a distasteful kind, infinite offense caused to respectable families in the neighborhood—"

"Turnips and stuffed shirts."

"You are not fit to tie their bootlaces," said my grandpapa, who had a grand way with clichés. "If you do not agree to marry, and marry sensibly and well, the alternative will be to give you a fixed allowance with the sternest warning that this you must manage yourself, and that no new debts will on any account be settled by me or by the Bank."

There was a silence while this was considered.

"Oh? And what sort of sum were you thinking of for this allowance?"

There was a further pause, intended to be impressive.

"We were thinking of the sum of one thousand pounds per annum."

There was a great yelp of laughter, and the sound of a chair being pushed back.

"I thought this was meant to be a serious discussion. I might as well be on my way. Pleasure calls!"

"You can mock!" said my grandfather's weighty tones. "But think over what we have said, or it will be infinitely the worse for you. I cannot imagine what any man could have against marrying a sweet girl like one of the Coverdales, or one of the Blacketts."

"Mary Coverdale is a very pretty girl" came my uncle Frank's voice from over by the door. "I know many pretty girls."

There was the sound of a door slamming, then sounds of the family conference breaking up in what was the nearest the Fearings could get to disorder. I retreated to my hopping game, but I was mentally composing a new skipping rhyme:

Sarah, Jane, and Clare and Mary,
Auntie Mary is no fairy.

I had never to my knowledge seen Mary Coverdale, and had no idea whether she was a large young lady. It didn't sound like it, but truth had very little to do with my skipping games. I might in time find a better rhyme for Mary. My mother's name, by the way, was Harriet, as you've heard, and the only reason I didn't include her in the games was that the one rhyme I could think of for it was "chariot,"and that didn't seem very fruitful.

I was hopping lonely as a cloud in the little courtyard that bordered the blank wall of the library when to my surprise I saw my mother. More surprising still, she and my father were walking together down the wide lawns constructed from the endless carts of earth brought to the site before ever a stone of Blakemere was laid, to improve its position and to provide beauteous gardens stretching down to the River Whate. They were walking and talking. Together.

My mother and my father never walked and talked together. They appeared together in public, at dinners and suchlike, when my mother did not cry off on grounds of poor health (that is, poor temper). On those occasions they had little to say to each other, in private still less. My mother, what is more, seldom left the house—seemed to dislike the open air. I watched, fascinated. After some minutes, as they seemed about to begin the descent to the river, my mother stopped, doubtless unwilling to contemplate the haul back up. They talked for a few moments longer. Then they paused, turned around toward the house, and saw me.

My mother looked straight ahead. At me and through me. My father's brow furrowed. Then they began talking again, and started off in my direction. Some yards away from the courtyard they paused again, my father making an earnest point. I was as sure as I could be that they were talking about me, but I went on hopping and jumping on my chalked squares on the courtyard. Then I heard my mother gulp, sob, and walk faster than was her wont in the direction of the East Door to the house.

My father watched his unloved and unloving wife for a moment or two, then shrugged. Her departure seemed to lift a weight off his shoulders. The furrowed expression went from his face, and he started toward me with a smile.

"And what are you up to, Sarah Jane?"

"Hopping . . . Papa."

"So I see. And what is the idea of it?"

I adopted a bored, explaining-the-obvious-to-adults tone.

"Well, you hop on *these* squares, then you come down with both feet on *these* squares, and you mustn't let your shoes touch the lines of the squares."

"I see. Like this?" And he poised himself at the starting point and went through a rough approximation of my game. "Was that right?"

"More or less," I conceded gracelessly. "But your feet touched the line lots of times."

"That's because my feet are bigger than yours. These squares are for delicate little girls' feet."

If he had been Uncle Frank I would have offered to draw a bigger set of squares beside mine, but as he was my father I didn't. We stood looking awkwardly at each other for a moment, at a loss for words with each other, as we always were. I was preparing to start hopping again when Papa unexpectedly said, "What would you say, Sarah Jane, if one day all this were yours?"

"All what?"

He waved grandly around.

"All this—house—grounds—"

This, I perceived, was a big matter.

"I'd say it was a very big house for a little girl."

My father shook his head.

"Oh, I'm thinking of far into the future. Of when you're grown up."

I considered further. Some faint breeze emanating from the women's suffrage movement, then still in its infancy, must have found its way into my schoolroom, for eventually I said stoutly, "I expect I could run it as well as any *boy*."

My father laughed. "Maybe you could, Sarah Jane. Maybe you could."

"But I would need to be much better taught than I am being at the moment."

He looked at me hard, his forehead furrowed again.

"It is a point to be considered. Maybe I should consult with your grandmama."

And he resumed his walk back toward the East Door.

I now realize that it was on that day that my parents first really accepted the notion that I might be the eventual heir of Blakemere and of Fearing's Bank. It may even be that, as the family conference was breaking up, Grandpapa revealed the terms of his latest will for the first time. It would be nice to record that from that day my life changed, but it did not. My mother still ignored my existence, and my father still looked as if he couldn't remember who I was if he came upon me unexpectedly.

But my governess of the moment was sent packing, and shortly afterward Miss Roxby arrived, and stayed with me until I was seventeen.

As my father walked away, I resumed my game, and thought no more of the matter. My mind was on Uncle Frank. How wonderful he had been, standing up to the combined weight and might of the rest of the family! "Outface" was a word I had learned recently, and I was sure he had outfaced them. A thousand pounds a year sounded an awful lot to my young ears, but it was clear that nobody—no young man of family—could be expected to live on it. It must have been not long after this that I informed a young friend that "No gentleman could be expected to live on less than five thousand a year." He was the son of one of the undergardeners, and he reminded me of the remark quite often in later years.

I was sure my uncle Frank was right not to marry if he didn't want to marry. Why should such a splendid man take a wife chosen for him by his family? Uncle Frank could have any woman he wanted, any woman in the world. I rather think the idea occurred to me that if he would only wait, say, ten years, he could have me.

CHAPTER THREE

Edging Toward the Abyss

My uncle Frank was the center of my life. Perhaps you will have guessed that already. At the time of Mr. Gladstone's visit he was a shining figure who brought fun from time to time into my rather shadowy existence. By the time of the overheard family conference he was the only being in my family I loved, and for that reason the love was passionate, singleminded, overmastering. His visits to Blakemere were occasional, but as soon as I got the slightest hint that there was one in prospect I was afire with anticipation, and he never disappointed me. I was the first one he asked for, though he never needed to do that: I was lurking somewhere—behind one of the marble balustrades above the entrance hall, or peering through a crack in the open door leading to the Blue Salon. The moment he asked, I would fly to his arms—to be lifted aloft, kissed, asked what I was doing, asked who my new governess was, tickled, *loved*.

The truthful answer to the question what I had been doing would have been "existing without you," but I was not mature enough to frame such an answer or to understand my emotional state. By the time I did understand it, Uncle Frank was gone forever. As it was, I told him such of my little doings as I thought might interest him, invented others, and generally took him over for the length of his visit. I now realize I could do that because there were few competing attractions, but at the time I only knew that he loved me, and that his visits transformed the gloomy vastness of Blakemere into a heaven.

At the time of the Gladstone visit my most dearly dear uncle was still a favored son, his eccentricities indulged because he represented the best hope of a male heir for Blakemere, and for Fearing's Bank. By the time of the family conference, patience was wearing thin, and he was beginning to be regarded as a black sheep. But then, patience was not a family trait, and it was altogether in character that they should make him into what they feared he was becoming. Even my grandmother, wisest of the clan, was someone with strict standards, definite expectations, and with impatience for those who lived otherwise than as she would have wished. "Slack" was a word she used often, and "not up to par." Uncle Frank incurred these terrible judgments all too frequently. His debts were hardly enormous, were eminently settleable, granted the size of the family fortune, but they were as unacceptable to my grandmother as to everyone else at Blakemere. In 1884, he sat close to Grandpapa entertaining Mr. Gladstone (no easy task, I imagine). By 1890, he was, metaphorically at least, below the salt, even out in the cold.

"They want me to be a nine-to-five person," he told me one day when we were fishing together two miles down the River Whate but still within sight of the enormous pile that was Blakemere. "They want a glorified bank clerk. I'm damned if they're going to get one in me."

One of the (many) attractions of Uncle Frank was that he swore in my presence.

I nodded solemnly. "They should give you the wherewithal"—(I loved words like that)—"to live the sort of life you want to live."

Uncle Frank let out one of his great laughs. "How right you are, little rabbit! But you're biased, aren't you—you and I being great chums. I don't think anyone would agree with you *up there*."

And he jerked his thumb in the direction of the great lump of masonry that we never seemed able to escape from.

"I don't suppose they would," I said firmly, dissociating myself from

Blakemere, and from all it stood for. "But you mustn't let them wear you down."

"Oh, they'll wear me down in the long run," said Uncle Frank, making me very sad, because I had something of the same feeling. "So maybe I should have a really big fling before they bring me into line, eh?"

I considered this.

"Does that mean that in the end you'll be forced to marry this Miss Coverdale?"

"How did *you* hear about Miss Coverdale?" he asked, turning and looking at me, astonished.

"I *over*heard," I said truthfully. "Does it?"

"Miss Coverdale, Miss Blackett, Miss Waddington-Phipps, Miss This-or-That—what does it matter who? It may as well be Miss Coverdale as any other. Yes, I suppose so. They'll win in the end, and Blakemere will demand an heir, to prevent the dreadful fate of its falling into female hands."

"Yes, I overheard that, too."

"Do you mind?" he asked, turning and looking into my face.

"You having a son? Not at all. Daddy sort of asked me, and I had to say girls ought to be the same as boys, of course—"

"Of *course*," Uncle Frank said gravely.

"But really I can't imagine anything more horrible than inheriting Blakemere, though I didn't tell Papa that." I thought, and then added, "But I think you should marry who you want to marry."

"Not too easy, that, if you don't care to marry at all. But if that is to be my fate, I rather think I'll have a little fling first—no, a great big one!"

"Another of your expeditions, do you mean?"

"Another of them, yes. Crossing the Sahara. Or maybe the Gobi Desert."

"Are all expeditions terribly costly?"

"Mine are! And this one will be terribly, terribly so. One day I'll take you with me on one."

The prospect thrilled me indescribably.

"*Will you*? Across the Gobi Desert?"

"Maybe not that. I don't think the Gobi Desert is the sort of place for a lady to go to. We'll stick to Europe. I'll take you to Eastern Europe—Athens, Tirana, Sofia, Bucharest: places where the Ottomans used to hold sway."

I frowned.

"I thought an Ottoman was a funny sort of sofa."

"Turks, then. The emperors who rule from Constantinople, a vast Moslem empire."

"Moslem? Does that mean they are heretics?"

"They are heretics to us, and we are heretics to them. Remember that."

I considered the thought.

"Do all religions consider other religions he-re—he-re—"

"Her*et*ical. Yes, I'm afraid so. It says very little for religious people, in my opinion. Before we in our family use words like that, we should remember that your grandmama's father was a heretic before he . . . came over to Christianity."

There was a strong implication, which I caught, that my great-grandfather had become a Christian for unworthy and self-interested motives, and that he would have done very much better to stay where he was as far as religion was concerned. This is one of my dear uncle Frank's opinions which has remained with me for life, though I have never ceased to be a Christian of sorts myself.

"I don't suppose," I said wistfully, as we gathered up our bait and tackle and started back to our marble prison, "that you will be able to send me letters from the Gobi Desert?"

"I'm afraid not," said Uncle Frank gently. "Not even one of these picture postcards you are so fond of."

"What will I *do*, all those months when you're away?"

"Perhaps you could get Miss Roxby to plot a course across the Gobi Desert from Kanchow to Ulan Bator, at about twenty miles a day. Then you can stick pins into it every morning and imagine roughly where we are and roughly when we shall start back. But remember, Sarah Jane—"

"Yes?"

"Not a word to anyone till I set off. It's a secret, little rabbit." We were rounding the below-stairs part of Blakemere, the prison's dungeon, so to speak, but one from which delicious smells often emanated. "Twitch your nose, little rabbit."

It was the reason for his nickname for me. That day the smell was wonderful.

"How *lucky* you are, to eat something that smells like that," I said. "In the nursery it will certainly be boiled mince and a milk pudding."

It was. But I was nourishing in my childish bosom the secret which he had entrusted to me, so I ate it stoically. It was typical of Uncle Frank that he should lighten the burden of his absence by making it a delightful secret, typical of me that I should keep it faithfully. There was no one in the family I would want to entrust it to, and this made me congenitally mistrustful. For that reason it was seldom that I confided anything of importance to Beatrice or Miss Roxby, my new governess. Miss Roxby was well read for a governess. Her mother had imprudently married an actor, and had warned her against contracting an alliance based on personal attractions (unnecessarily, or so it seemed at the time). We neither of us found it easy to express emotions, though I had a great respect for her—and, eventually, she for me.

The double joy of a secret is that you can not only hug it to yourself while it *is* a secret, but when it comes out, you can reveal that you have known it all along. Providence, not generally kind to me during my childhood, gave me that second joy in good measure. I remember it as about a month after Frank's leaving Blakemere that we heard from him, but perhaps it was longer: he had, after all, an expedition to prepare. It was late in the day and Miss Roxby and I had just come in from some botanical excursion in a distant corner of the prison compound when my father and grandfather arrived back from a day at the Bank in London. Grandpapa, as was his custom, took up the evening post that was lying on a silver salver on the fat-legged marble table nearest the large double-doored entrance. He riffled through them, then brought one up close to his old eyes.

"Your brother Frank's writing," he spluttered to my father. "From Port Said."

My father said nothing, but stood there waiting. I never quite knew what his attitude to his brother was. I did not see him often enough to have the information.

"The damn fool! He's got up another of his preposterous expeditions—to cross the Gobi Desert!" said my grandfather in a voice of outrage.

"Oh, I knew *that*," I said loudly. For once I was the center of attention.

"You knew?" said my father.

"Of course. From Kanchow to Ulan Bator." I turned to Miss Roxby. "He said you would help me to chart his progress."

Miss Roxby blenched. I don't think she was terribly well up in the Gobi Desert.

"Why didn't you tell anyone," demanded my father.

"Who?" I asked, to underline my solitary state. "Anyway, I thought everybody knew."

I was a truthful child as a rule, but my probity had its limits. I turned from their gaze and toiled up the stairs with Miss Roxby. I did not tell them that Uncle Frank had said he might be willing to marry Miss Coverdale when he came home. This, I thought, was part of the secret I had been sworn to keep. Anyway, he might have changed his mind when he returned, and decided to wait for me.

Miss Roxby was nothing if not industrious. Within a week she had procured from among the unread volumes in the irrelevant library a large, dusty, and leather-bound tome with an unmanageable folding-out map of China and Mongolia. This was to be our Sacred Book for the next few months. From the letter from Port Said she had tried to calculate Uncle Frank's likely date of arrival in Shanghai, so we could talk till then of his possible ports of call, before we discussed his overland route across the dreadfully inhospitable landscape—that slow, painful journey of twenty miles a day to Ulan Bator.

The fact that all our calculations were grossly inaccurate does not lessen my gratitude to her: our discussions and fantasies were the one thing that lightened the burden of the long months of separation. As I sit here in the gatehouse, enjoying the long summer evenings, I remember fantasies I indulged in with particular pleasure. They included a romance for Uncle Frank, in the middle of the desert, with a Mongolian lady dressed in improbably bright clothing, facially somewhere between a Japanese geisha and an illustration in one of my books of Pokahontas. Uncle Frank also rescued other members of his expedition from terrible dangers, and repulsed single-handed marauding parties of Mongolians, eventually running up the Union Jack at the desert's central point and claiming it for Queen Victoria. Thinking of the problems we have at the moment in India and various other parts of what used to be the Empire, it is perhaps fortunate that Uncle Frank refrained from prizing Outer Mongolia from the grips of whoever then ruled it to add to them.

It was not summer but late autumn when Uncle Frank arrived home. There had been, as always, no advance notice. He may have felt that any letter would only come by sea, like himself, so it could hardly arrive much before him, though in fact he later told me he had had a week in Cairo ("sampling the fleshpots," he said, which made me wonder whether the Egyptians were cannibals) on the way home.

It was not surprising that I was the first to know of his return, since whenever I passed a window which looked out over the long drive that led to the Gatehouse and beyond that to the little country village of Melbury I scanned the rolling expanses of Fearing property for signs of Uncle Frank's return. And when one day in early October I saw the carriage that plied between Melbury station and residences of consequence in the neighborhood I knew at once that it contained my dear uncle. This was not childish intuition. I had been wrong a hundred times before, and eventually I had to be right. I left Miss Roxby's side and tumbled down the marble staircase (each step better adapted to a fully fledged giant than to my by-now eleven-year-old legs), and positioned myself in a dismal alcove containing the sort of sinister potted plant that thrives on shadow. If he had known it was Uncle Frank arriving, Mr. McKay would certainly have been there in the echoing entrance hall, his face set in just the right blend of welcome and disapproval. As it was, there was just Robert, an underfootman, his face blank not from formality but from boredom.

This was not a time for coyness or for playing games. The moment

I saw the weatherbeaten face below the panama hat, I rushed from my hiding place.

"Uncle Frank! Uncle Frank!"

He swung me aloft, my beribboned hair knocking off his fine hat, and he kissed me and tickled me and roared his delight at seeing me again.

"Sarah Jane! The only thing worth coming home for!"

That made me swell with delight and pride. When the boisterous part of the welcome was over, he put me down on the staircase, sat down beside me and looked at me closely.

"How you've grown. You'll soon be a full-sized rabbit. I won't be able to swing you up in my arms much longer."

"I shall be a young lady," I said roguishly, "and it won't be proper for you to swing me up."

"How true. The dignity of young ladies must be preserved. Be glad you're not a Chinese lady who has to walk a respectful distance behind her menfolk."

"Does she *really*? I thought that was only in books. It can't make for stimulating conversation. Anyway, I don't have any menfolk."

"You have me. And I've never noticed you being particularly respectful of me."

"Would you want me to be?"

He laughed, throwing his head back. "You know, come to think of it, I don't think I would like that at all."

"Be careful you don't take cold, Sarah Jane," my governess said quietly from two steps above us. And the stair was rather chilly through my dress and light undergarments. Uncle Frank stood up and turned around.

"How right you are, Miss—er, Roxby, isn't it?" He looked at her quizzically and appraisingly (I can see the expression now, and can analyze it, though I could not have done so then. He was wondering whether she was an ally or a foe). "I trust your charge has grown in knowledge and wisdom as much as she has grown in stature during my absence?"

I giggled. "She had increased her knowledge of Outer Mongolia quite prodigiously," said Miss Roxby gravely. "But I hope she has learned a lot of other useful things as well."

"I am delighted to hear it. Ah well, now for the difficult bit," said Uncle Frank, his shoulders shrugging underneath his magnificent traveling coat. "Pleasant things never last, do they? But one who has braved the present-day descendants of Ghengis Khan should not shrink from being taken back into the bosom of his family, should he?"

And he kissed me again, shook hands ceremoniously with Miss Roxby, and took himself off into the gloomy body of the house. I heard no whoops of joy at his return.

In the next few days I went to great lengths to find out what was *going on*—about my uncle Frank's debts, his way of life, above all about his proposed marriage. This was not easy: Miss Roxby kept better surveillance over me than my earlier governesses, and the family did not have the aristocratic insouciance that would have allowed them to have family rows in front of the servants (of whom Miss Roxby was certainly one). This meant that my play times were spent in tracking down members of the family who might be consulting together about the Frank problem. Alas, in the daytime they never were, or if they were, it was in totally inaccessible or unguessable parts of the house, which had many such. When I saw Uncle Frank with the family his manner was always nonchalant, uncowed. In fact, he almost seemed to be tormenting them.

"What is a gay bachelor to do on a dull November day in the country?" he would say to his mother. "I must teach one of the footmen to play billiards."

His mother compressed her lips, sensible enough not to point out that if he did what the family wanted him to, he wouldn't be a bachelor at all.

"What you should do with me, you know, is lock me up in a small, obscure room in this rotten pile," I heard him say to my father, "and have the servants bring me some basic meals three times a day, and then you'd be rid of all the worry and expense of me. You could give it out I'd lost my reason. The mad brother in the attic—I have rather a fancy for the role. And the whole county would believe it. They would believe any rumor about me, provided it was bad enough. Maybe after a while I could get out, roam the house by the light of a candle and burn it down. Take more than a candle to do that, though, I would imagine."

There was no reply to this from my father. I think he was in two minds about the family's determination to get Uncle Frank married. Quite apart from the prospect of my inheriting Blakemere, there was the possibility of Mama dying and of his marrying again and fathering a son (though on reflection I don't think Papa was particularly philoprogenitive).

But the most memorable example of Frank's teasing his family occurred one morning when Miss Roxby and I were proceeding downstairs (a major operation in itself) to go out for our walk, needing some fresh air between Arithmetic and French. We looked down, hearing voices, and we saw Frank encountering his father in the entrance hall. My uncle was smartly and rather formally dressed, the carriage drawn up outside the door.

"Must pay my respects to the neighbors now I'm home again," he said cheerily. "They'll expect to hear my account of remote parts."

"Splendid, splendid," said Grandpapa.

"I've always been on excellent terms with the . . . Blacketts," said Uncle Frank over his shoulder as he made his exit to the waiting carriage.

Grandpapa's face fell. He knew he was being played with, but he'd hoped that his son was visiting the Coverdales. But I knew, and I knew because Miss Roxby knew, and Miss Roxby knew because her best friend was governess at the Blacketts, that Mary Coverdale's best friend was Violet Blackett, and if she was to be found anywhere during the day away from her own home, it would be Matton Hall, the Blacketts' country seat.

As the carriage drove away, as jaunty in its motion as Uncle Frank's own walk, I felt a tear come into my eye at the thought that he had been defeated. Now, nearly sixty years later, he seems in my memory to have been walking to his doom.

CHAPTER FOUR

THE CHINA ROSE

I could barely contain my impatience for Uncle Frank's return from his visit to the Blacketts'. I calculated the distance, the likely length of the visit, and I could only hope that his return would coincide with one of the free half-hours I was allowed during the day. For the rest of the time I gave what attention I could to the French pluperfect tense and the Peasants' Revolt of 1381. Alas, the midafternoon break passed without any sign of Uncle Frank, and so did the break at the end of the day's lessons. I was reduced to asking Mr. McKay if he had returned, to be told that he had not.

My nursery supper consisted of Irish stew (very superior Irish stew, but I often wondered if the Irish ever ate anything else, because I never heard of any other dish originating in that country), and a very boring trifle. After it, I was at liberty for an hour, and normally I would have read, for I was developing a taste for novels that has never left me. However, I resisted the call of *Under Two Flags* or *A Study in Scarlet*, for there was a stronger pull on me. I went and stood inside the doorway of a little upstairs sitting room called the Peacock Room (nasty birds, nasty room). It was gaudy but never used, like so much of the house, and merely the dumping place for the less prestigious pictures, statuary, and furniture the family had accumulated.

It was cold there, but I stood steadfastly in the shadow as the family dinner hour approached, prepared to fade into the darkness if the footsteps along the corridor were my father's, or my aunt Jane's, or to slip out and pull him in if they were my uncle Frank's.

When at last he came, hurrying because he was late, but looking wonderfully handsome in his evening clothes, I materialized before his surprised eyes in the corridor and pulled him into the dim shadows of the Peacock Room.

"Well?" I said.

"Well what, little rabbit?"

"You know very well, Uncle Frank, so please don't play games."

"I know nothing at all of what you're talking about, and I'm late for dinner."

"You never mind being late for dinner. Did you meet Mary Coverdale on your visit to the Blacketts?"

(You will perceive I was rather a bossy and peremptory child. I have had traces of these traits all my life, or so people tell me.)

"Mary Coverdale . . . Mary Coverdale . . ." Uncle Frank stroked his light-brown beard, his eyes twinkling. "Yes, now you mention it, I think there *was* someone of that name."

I got quite annoyed, for once, at those eyes twinkling at me in the gloomy half-light.

"Don't play with me! What is she like?"

"Ah—you tax my powers of description . . ." Uncle Frank pretended it was hard to remember. "Quite tall, for a young lady . . . excellent figure, just the right balance between slim and full . . . dressed with taste—even I could see that . . ."

"You haven't mentioned her face."

"Have I not? Exquisite complexion, like fine china, rosebud mouth, hazel eyes—quite the English rose."

I considered.

"I'm not sure I like the English rose type."

"Well, you wouldn't," said Uncle Frank brutally, "not being the English rose type yourself."

"Oh? And what type am I?"

"The rose of Sharon, I should say."

And while I was considering what he could mean by this, he made his escape.

Later that evening, as the hour for bed approached, Miss Roxby noticed something about me and commented, "You seem very excited this evening, Sarah."

"Excited, Miss Roxby?"

"Well, tense. As if there is something on your mind."

"I don't know why that should be."

I had all the stonewalling arts of a politician, you notice. I did not, at that stage in my young life, confide in Miss Roxby. But I did feel a debt of gratitude to her, and I did not like to snub her. Some minutes later, I said, "What is the rose of Sharon, Miss Roxby?"

" 'I am the rose of Sharon, and the lily of the valleys.' It's the Bible, Sarah."

I often wondered where Miss Roxby got her knowledge of the Bible from, since she often confided in me that neither her papa nor her mama was religious. I conjectured an *affaire* with a student of theology.

"I see. And what would that mean if someone compared you to a rose of Sharon?"

Her eyes twinkled. "Your uncle Frank, I presume? Well, I suppose he means you are a Jewish sort of rose—more like your grandmama than some of the other members of your family."

I considered the idea and felt pleased by it. I admired my grandmother. She wasn't particularly kind to me in any way, paid me no special attention, but I knew instinctively that she was clever, and it pleased me to be thought clever, too. I did not think that English roses were clever.

"What part of the Bible does that come from, Miss Roxby?"

"*The Song of Solomon.*"

"Can we read it together?"

"When you are older, Sarah."

I digested this piece of information, too, but with difficulty. This was the first time I had had any intimation that there are parts of the Bible that one does not read until one is older. I knew that was true of novels such as *Jane Eyre* and *Tom Jones*, but—the Bible? It made me intensely curious as to what Solomon was singing about.

After that day, Uncle Frank's courtship proceeded—but it would be wrong to suggest that it proceeded "apace," or smoothly, or in any other of the ordinary ways that would be expected from a dull, everyday young man. Uncle Frank enjoyed tormenting his family too much to behave conventionally. Days would pass without his taking a step in the direction of the Coverdales' manor house, Tillyards. Or he would disappear for a whole day, and when he caught an expectant eye on him on his return, reveal that he had been over to a friend's for a spot of shooting. Or he would make derogatory remarks about Mary Coverdale—her literary tastes, her frocks, even her person ("her shoulders are like a brewery drayman's" he said once, and even I was shocked).

"Don't you *like* Miss Coverdale?" I asked, unable probably to keep the hopefulness out of my voice.

"She is *Mary* Coverdale," he said, prevaricating, and puffing a great cloud of cigar smoke in my direction. "Her elder sister is *Miss* Coverdale."

I waited, but there was no continuation.

"Don't you like *Mary* Coverdale," I was forced to ask.

"Oh, I've no doubt she'll do well enough," he replied. "And that's all the reply you're getting, little rabbit."

"I'm too old to be called 'little rabbit'," I objected.

He gave me a long look.

"I rather think you are right," he said.

But in spite of that long look, he took himself over to the Coverdales' next day.

Eventually, in spite of the lackadaisical nature of my uncle Frank's wooing, things inevitably started working toward an understanding between the two families. I heard of the next stage from Beatrice, my best friend in the house.

"A visit is to be paid," she said significantly.

I considered the matter.

"By us or by them?"

"By them. Her father, mother, brother, and her younger sister."

"And her."

"Of course and her. On Saturday week."

"What will they do, Bea?" I wondered. "Family visits are all very well in summer, but in the middle of February?"

"A dinner would be easier," agreed Beatrice. "But this is going to be an all-day visit."

"Will they bring their servants?"

"Some," said Beatrice. She felt my eyes on her. "And curiosity killed the cat, Sarah Jane."

I knew that Tom, the coachman at Tillyards, the Coverdale manor house, was "sweet" on Beatrice. At that date, the lower orders, when moving toward marriage, were always said to be "sweet" on each other. I didn't get the impression that Tom was in any way sweet—his appeal to Beatrice was that of a manly man with decisive ways. He was also some years older than she was.

My doubts about Blakemere as a setting for a family visit were beyond my years, but perfectly natural. Though it was the sleeping and eating place of so many of the Fearings, it did not have the feel of a family home. It was more a sort of mansion branch of Fearing's Bank, a financial rather than a familial center. Its marbled, over-decorated immensity could never in any circumstance comprise the intimacy which is a part of the general understanding of the word "home." There are royal palaces which are cozier.

Blakemere was not a place where adults amused themselves either, but it did have the capacity for amusement. There was more than one billiard room, for example, and in the Green Drawing Room there was a quite remarkably ugly ormolu chess set, which normally functioned as an occasional table, but the top of which could be swung over, to reveal a checkered board and a collection of aggressive figures like malignant dwarfs, of which the Queen was quite the most hideous.

I was not, of course, part of the preparations for the Coverdale visit, but I was to be part of the event, and lessons were to be suspended for the day. The Coverdales had had three girls, the eldest of whom was now married to a minor functionary in the Diplomatic Service and was currently with him in St. Petersburg. They had then had a boy, and decided to call it a day. Two boys would have been more prudent. Peter, the son, joined the Army and was killed in the early months of the Great War. Tillyards, a beautiful Elizabethan manor house, became a school when Peter's father died, and is now little better than a ruin.

"You, Sarah Jane, go to the end of the line with Miss Roxby behind you," said my grandfather, gesturing.

"It's *Sarah*," I muttered, under my breath. It sounded much more grown up, but so far I had persuaded only Miss Roxby and Uncle Frank to adopt the shorter version.

We were all standing on the magnificent low steps at the main entrance to Blakemere Manor, looking as if we were posing for a photographer in the manner we chose to send down to posterity. It was not the way I would want to be welcomed to a house, I thought. Once we were in position there was little we could do but wait. Collectively we had very little conversation. The servants, standing to the side of the steps (out of camera range, so to speak), had duties assigned to them when the Coverdales arrived, so they were more natural. We shifted uneasily from foot to foot. Eventually two carriages were sighted, a mile away down the endless drive, and we watched in silence as the two specters gradually assumed recognizable shapes and finally drew up before the grand entrance to Blakemere. In the first carriage were Sir Thomas and Lady Coverdale, with a maid and a man; in the second, the three members of the younger generation, with a maid for the girls. There was no doubting the friendliness with which my grandparents and my papa greeted the senior Coverdales, but I was interested only in the second coach, and only in the girls therein. They were both well-grown, attractive young women, and one could not tell who was the youngest from their looks alone. But one was kissed by my grandfather as a valued neighbor, the other was kissed as a future member of the family.

"Mary!" he said. "It does my heart good to see you here."

It didn't do my heart good, but I did look at her as dispassionately as possible. The initial, fleeting impression was much as Uncle Frank had suggested: flawless complexion, beautiful auburn hair, rosebud mouth with a little bow top to it, charmingly simple dress under her handsome coat with the fur collar.

Then Uncle Frank came forward, shook hands with her coolly, and they started together into the house.

"Sarah Jane, I'm sure Peter would like to see the grounds," said my grandmother.

I looked up at Peter Coverdale's face. He was fifteen, and probably bitterly resented being entrusted to the care of a twelve-year-old girl. But he shrugged a sort of agreement, and we began the long trek round to the side of our monstrous pile, then on to the formal gardens at the back, with their close-clipped hedges, their graded terraces filled with regimented shrubs, and beyond that, the (artificial) meadows that sloped down to the river. As we mooched around the top terrace, speechless, Peter stopped at one point and turned to look at the house.

"I say, isn't it horrid!" he said.

"Hideous!" I agreed. We both laughed. It was a defining moment, a sort of liberation for me. None of the gardeners' children would have said that. From then on, Peter and I got on quite well, in spite of that terrible three-year age gap. "I'm sure Tillyards is much nicer," I said.

He shrugged. "It's not bad. I'm going into the Army."

This suggested a new idea to me.

"You mean you don't want to inherit it?"

"Not particularly."

"Could you refuse it?"

"More or less. I could just let it out to someone. Plenty of rich Jews wanting country houses."

I tactfully did not point out our Jewish connections.

"If Uncle Frank doesn't have a son, this will be mine."

"Yours? But you're a girl."

I nodded, unrebelliously. "But that's what grandpapa's will says. We only have quite distant cousins who are boys—apart from Aunt Clare's, and she married beneath her."

Peter Coverdale looked at the pile again, and whistled. "Well, if I were you I'd emigrate to Patagonia before I took on responsibility for a dump like that."

"I think you're probably quite right," I said.

But I enjoyed greatly showing him round, and hearing his derogatory comments on everything. If my grandmother's aim was to get us interested in each other, she certainly failed (he was not Uncle Frank, or even like him in temperament), but I came to like him a lot, was always interested in his career, and wept at his death. We sat together at lunch, and he whispered to me about the massed battalions of servants, the assertively beflowered china, and the hideous, twisted silverware: "like two elderly wrestlers grappling with each other" was how he rather daringly described a fruit stand with myriad bowls of pineapples, apricots, and grapes from the hothouse.

But my main interest at lunch was his sister Mary, of course. She was sitting five places down on the other side of the table, next to Uncle Frank, naturally. He was paying her an attention that was a long way short of assiduous but rather more than casual. He could do that sort of thing with an off-hand charm that was part of his nature. She was accepting it coolly for what it was, though with the occasional flirtatious gesture that showed she knew what the marriage game was, and perhaps had played it before. There was a confidence about her, about her way of looking around the Dining Room as if she already had a part stake in it that repelled me. But then, I was very ready to be repelled.

She was lovely, I had to admit, with the loveliness one saw on biscuit tins, on postcard series of "British beauties," or in pictures in the *Illustrated London News* showing Society ladies in the Prince of Wales's circle. But there was one occasion during lunch when she looked in our direction—not at me, for I had no place in her scheme of things, was to be annihilated by it—and I caught the expression in her eyes; it was one of cold, hard calculation.

"Is your sister nice?" I asked Peter, with assumed childishness.

"She'll save you from *this*," he said significantly.

After lunch, which was ostentatiously simple (no rich, elaborate dishes, but everything out of season yet of supreme quality) the party separated for various pursuits—several of the ladies forming a card party around my grandmother, men playing the inevitable billiards, Frank and Mary going for the standard tour of the grounds, and so on. I told Peter about our new acquisition of a Ping-Pong table, and he was wild for a game.

"I've heard of it," he said, "but I've never even seen it played."

It was while I was going for the bats and balls that I caught a glimpse of Peter's father, Sir Thomas. He had been left on his own for a moment by Grandpapa, and he was walking along the picture gallery, surveying the Italian paintings which were our most prestigious acquisition, rubbing his hands the while. He clearly appreciated the value, if not the beauty, of pictures. He had a little goatee beard and a watery but rapacious eye. He reminded me rather of the unsalubrious last Emperor of the French, whose widow had visited Blakemere two years before. I thought that Peter's instinct to get away from his family was a wise one. I thought that our growing involvement with them was a terrible mistake—though how terrible I could not then guess.

I was marginal to the visit, and so was Peter. Most of what I remember from the rest of the day was the Ping-Pong, and Peter's joy at the fastness of it, and the glorious sound of the ball on the table. Though I had played often with one of the gardeners' sons of my own age, Peter soon beat me, from his superior height and quickness.

"If *only* I could persuade my father to buy a table," he lamented, as we paused between games.

"He doesn't *look* as if he likes buying things like that," I said.

"He doesn't."

"You can come here and play whenever you like," I said expansively.

He looked around disparagingly.

"It's not the sort of place you can descend on with a party of your chums, is it?"

That summed up Blakemere, and also put me in my place. But I already knew the place of twelve-year-old girls, however filthy rich, in the world view of fifteen-year-old boys.

That day made two marriages and sealed the fates of four people. One marriage was actually agreed and arranged that day. I saw my friend Beatrice and Tom South the coachman at Tillyards walking hand in hand in the kitchen garden—he large and wreathed in smiles, she pensive but not unhappy. Soon she was to go out of my daily life, though certainly not out of my life as a whole, for she visited and I visited whenever we could, and I knew the story of her marriage from its hopeful start to its dismal end.

I was talking the other day to Gabriel South, her youngest son, about his parents' marriage. He is the Labour Party's agent for Bedford, and likely to be an MP as soon as there is a seat vacant in the area.

"You mustn't think the faults were all on the one side," he said. "You think that because you only ever saw my mother, and you loved her. I sometimes think she only married him to have children, and thought his proposal might be her last chance. They had nothing at all in common, lived in separate worlds. He was all physical, loved horses and shooting and playing cricket and football. She was for reading and self-education, as you know, and thank God for that. But there was nowhere for them to come together. It was a mismatch from the start."

That last judgment could be made on the other pair whose fate was sealed that day. Uncle Frank did not actually propose during the visit—that wasn't his way, to do the expected or the hoped-for. It was a full month before he proposed, was accepted, and the engagement was announced in the *Morning Post*. But the die was cast that day, the match became for him inescapable. I was watching from the library as they came in from their promenade around the grounds. Mary Coverdale's cold eyes were aglint with triumph as she surveyed the magnificent expanse of her future domain. Uncle Frank seemed somehow smaller, and his eyes were entirely blank.

CHAPTER FIVE

The Wedding

In the four months between the announcement of the engagement and the wedding I behaved abominably. Someone observing me today would assuredly diagnose a bad case of sexual jealousy. My generation heard excitedly of Sigmund Freud, discussed fragments of his theories as they were ignorantly reported in polite society, and developed a terrible mishmash of ideas based on them. The generation succeeding mine swallowed him wholesale. We live in an age of Freudianism reduced to cliché.

Nevertheless, I would contend, even at this date, that the diagnosis would be wrong, at least as far as the predominant strand of my feelings about the marriage was concerned. I had a child's passionate feelings for justice (I hope and believe it has never left me), and it seemed to me simply *wrong* that Uncle Frank should be pressured into making a marriage that was against his inclinations. My views of marriage were a good deal more romantic than the prevalent view in either the banking or the aristocratic circles in which we moved. The idea that, in allowing himself to be pressured into marriage as he had been, my uncle cut a less than heroic figure was not one that occurred to me, or that I would have admitted if it had.

The fact that, three weeks before Uncle Frank's marriage, I was to lose Beatrice to her coachman only increased my desolation and worsened my behavior. My life was dominated by a dreadful sense of loss.

Therefore, when I misbehaved, when I had tantrums, screamed "It's not fair!" to the heedless winds, refused to eat, got my clothes filthy in the grounds, and displayed my slovenliness for family and guests to wonder at, there was no one whom I loved to coax me into a more amenable frame of mind. Beatrice, to be sure, gave me what time she could, but her mind was already on future children for whom I was merely a foreshadowing and a substitute. Uncle Frank was rarely at Blakemere (which did not mean he was necessarily at Tillyards with his bride-to-be), and when he was, his notice of me was more off-handed, as a consequence of his preoccupied state of mind—and perhaps, I now think, of some feelings of shame.

Mary Coverdale, when she came to Blakemere, treated me as she meant to treat me when she came into her future state: that is, she ignored me. I was an irrelevance, and future sons would render my insignificance even more palpable.

Inevitably I was asked to be one of the bridesmaids—no, was told I was to be one of them.

"I refuse," I said.

My words, repeated as often as the subject was brought up, took on a heroic ring in my ears. So much more dignified and principled than a mere "no," I thought. In time the words began to rank in my egotistical imagination with Martin Luther's "Here I stand" and Lars Porsena's oath that the great house of Tarquin should suffer wrong no more. A great deal of effort was put into making me change my mind—not by my mother, who put no effort into anything that concerned me, and not a great deal by my father, whose feelings about the marriage were ambiguous. But Aunt Jane, Grandmama, Beatrice (under pressure), and Aunt Sarah all tried. Grandmama was the most persuasive, the greatest danger.

"Your refusing will get the marriage off to a bad start, my dear," she said, when I had obeyed a rare summons to her own boudoir.

"It will start off badly in any case," I said.

"Nonsense, my dear. What can you know?"

"What could be a worse start than a bridegroom who is reluctant?" I asked, very conscious of right on my side.

"You've got a very silly idea into your head. Just look at how lovely your future aunt Mary is. It's a love match—everyone can see that."

"Uncle Frank is handsome as any man I've ever seen, but they can both be as lovely as anyone has ever been in the history of the world and still not be right for each other. Uncle Frank will go down the aisle as if he's being marched to the hangman's yard, and *I won't be part of it.*"

Finally I convinced them, and a daughter of Aunt Clare (and Uncle Alfred, though he was hardly ever mentioned at Blakemere) was drafted in to represent the Fearing family. This meant inviting both the child's parents to the wedding, which the family had hoped to avoid. However, a few weeks before the wedding, Uncle Alfred was elected to the Royal Academy (he was a very boring painter, though a charming man), and this meant that his profession could be mentioned when he was introduced to the other wedding guests, though some of the local gentry were still rather sniffy.

I was thrown during those weeks on the company of my governess Miss Roxby—Edith. With her I was petulant, indignant, openly contemptuous of the bargain that had been struck, but the worst of my tantrums and moods were controlled in her presence because I had come to respect her greatly, and because I sensed that she sympathized with my attitude to the marriage. She introduced me, in our spare time, to many books that have become lifelong friends, and she awoke in me an interest in my country's history which has been a great standby in my two main careers. I remember one occasion a few weeks before the wedding when I was questioning her about how the then Queen had come to the throne, and she had taken down a tall, heavy book full of photographs and engravings, which had been published for the Golden Jubilee (we were by then between Jubilees). It had a family tree of some complexity, and I studied it intently.

"So she inherited the throne," I said eventually, "even though her father's younger brothers had *sons*."

I had studied it, you see, with my own situation very much in my mind.

"That's right," said Edith Roxby. "If the Duke and Duchess of Kent had had a son, he would have taken precedence over the Princess Victoria, as she then was. But they didn't—he died soon after she was born—so she took precedence over the sons of his younger brothers."

"I see. That seems quite fair. . . . But it does seem odd that Uncle Frank should be badgered into marriage to produce a son."

"That is quite different, Sarah," said Miss Roxby, peddling the family line, I now know, with reluctance. "A son is needed to take over Fearing's Bank."

"So a woman may take over the country, but one may not take over Fearing's Bank?" I said, with remorseless logic. "Not that I *want* to! I can't think of anything more stuffy and tedious. But you'd think that what was good enough for the Royal Family would be good enough for Fearing's Bank, wouldn't you?"

Thus did the seeds sown by Mr. Gladstone's casual remark flourish in my childish brain.

As I have mentioned, there were occasions on which the happy bride-to-be Mary Coverdale visited Blakemere, and on such visits Uncle Frank (but she always called him Francis) was in attendance, glumly but dutifully. If she noticed his glumness she did not comment on it. She was not naturally a gay person herself. She had her mind set seriously on one subject, and went after it single-mindedly.

This was brought home to me forcibly by a scrap of conversation I overheard on one of those visits. As I have said, Mary Coverdale ignored me—not so much snubbing me as simply being unaware of my presence, since I had no place in her view of her own future at Blakemere. She was almost equally unaware of the existence of Aunt Jane and my mother, while being very conscious of the respect due to my grandfather and grandmother, and more uneasily aware of the claims of my father.

Anyway, the fact that I and Miss Roxby were also in the vicinity was ignored during one of these visits when Uncle Frank and his future bride were walking in the terrace gardens. They were arm-in-arm, yet they could not have seemed further apart. Miss Roxby and I were on a seat behind a hedge, studying a map of Africa showing how it had been opened up in recent years (by our heroic Empire builders, whose work will have to be comprehensively undone in the years ahead). As they passed by on the other side, I heard Uncle Frank mumble something into his beard—I imagine it was some professed doubt as to whether he could "make her happy." Mary Coverdale's voice came across the hedge to us clear as a silver spoon on fine glassware.

"You mustn't worry, Francis. We are extremely well suited. I shall be an excellent hostess for Blakemere."

They passed on. Miss Roxby looked at me and raised her eyebrows. Since she would never initiate such a conversation but sometimes allowed herself to be led into one, I said, "She doesn't understand the situation at all."

"Seemingly not," she said quietly.

"Uncle Frank doesn't care a fig for Blakemere, or for his wife being hostess here."

"I wouldn't have thought so."

"At least she doesn't imagine she is being married for love," I admitted grudgingly.

"True. And I suppose it will have been difficult for anyone to explain to her that she is being married in return for the wiping out of debts." She realized at once she had said too much, had given rein to a side of her that her profession obliged her to keep hidden. A child, however secretive by nature, could never entirely be trusted. She said quietly: "But to return to the Dark Continent . . ."

We were on our way to understanding each other very well indeed.

Meanwhile, preparations for the wedding were proceeding apace, though all the bride's preparations were going on at Tillyards, so I was not nauseated by them. The wedding was to be large, indisputably an event, but a local event. Uncle Frank had insisted on this latter point. I had heard him do this one day when, exceptionally, I was allowed to sit with the family at teatime. He made it clear he wanted none of the banking bigwigs from London invited, nor the national politicians.

"It is only the wedding of a younger son," he said. "To pretend otherwise would be tasteless."

He looked at my father when he said this.

"Don't expect me to back you up," Papa said. "It's a matter of indifference to me what sort of wedding you have."

"Nevertheless," said Uncle Frank carefully, "the fact is that circumstances could change, and you could be father to a whole string of future lairds of Blakemere."

My father's face twisted in distaste.

"I assure you that should circumstances change, as you so tactfully put it, the last thing I would consider would be to embark on a second venture of matrimony."

I rather pertly put in my two pennyworth: "And you needn't think I want to be Lairdess of Blakemere. I'm going to be a great writer."

Uncle Frank turned to me, with something of his old smile.

"Well, that's original, at any rate. We've never had a writer in the Fearing family."

"We've never had an explorer, either. I don't see why the Fearing family should produce nothing but bankers. I'm going to be a great writer, like the Brontë sisters."

"I won't have those women mentioned at my table!" thundered Grandpapa. I subsided into silence, but I noticed a satiric glint in my grandmother's eye. I think she knew that Grandpapa had very little idea who the Brontë sisters were, only that they were not quite respectable.

My ambition to be a writer, which lasted all of three months, at least made me observe the preparations and the wedding itself with an eye eager to absorb the telling details. I will not bore myself by setting them down—they would seem impossibly lavish and fussy in this Age of Austerity we live in now. Uncle Frank absented himself as far as possible from all the fuss and flurry. I imagine him as having several last flings in all his favorite bachelor haunts, though on second thought I don't imagine he saw them as last flings, and why on earth should he? Such a marriage as he was undertaking was not likely to change his essential nature, or his habits. It was like a royal marriage of convenience—like Charles II marrying a Portuguese princess he had never seen.

Finally the day dawned. I was not a bridesmaid, but I was not excused attending the awful event. My mother, of course, did not go. She had resisted all pressures to make preparations for it, saying that she had many dresses bought for other weddings she had not attended, and she would wear one of those if she was well enough to put in an appearance at Church. In the event she stayed in bed, as everyone knew she would. By this stage in her life she never did anything to please anyone other than herself. I saw her about once a month. I on the other hand was primped and prettified and eventually was taken in one of the family tumbrils to sit toward the back of the church with Miss Roxby, Aunt Clare and Uncle Alfred, and their three boys—those doubtful insurers of Fearing's Bank and its future. They were boisterous boys but pleasant enough, and they loathed the flummery of the wedding as much as I did, though for different reasons.

The church was St. Michael's at Great Orpenden. The family had no associations with the village, but it was the only church in the area large enough for the sort of grand wedding the family had planned (it was built in the fifteenth century to the glory of God and the woolen trade by one of the sleek profiteers of the time). Uncle Frank sat awaiting his blooming bride in the front pew, making no attempt to hide the fact that he would rather be anywhere else but here, doing anything else but this—a common enough feeling among bridegrooms, so it aroused little comment except some mild jocularities.

The bride, when she arrived, looked beautiful I had to admit—like a winter landscape in the sun. She walked slowly up the aisle to the usual musical accompaniments, attended by my cousin Kate, Aunt Clare's only female child, and various Coverdale girls, each one a biscuit-box picture in herself. Uncle Frank stood up, joined up with her as casually as if she were a lady he was meeting outside Swan and Edgar's, and went through his part of the ceremony with studied casualness, as if it was no part of the agreement he had entered into to pretend to take such nonsense seriously. Mary, on the other hand, was clear and word-perfect, a tribute to the elocution teacher's art. Eventually it was all over, and we got into the tumbrils again and returned to Blakemere for the festive baked meats.

I had hoped to slip away from there, but Miss Roxby was under strict instructions that I was to do the honors of the house to all the other children. This was something I was used to, though I never enjoyed it. Since most of the children there, including the Coverdale biscuit boxes, had been to Blakemere before, I confined myself to finding out what they wanted to do and providing them with the wherewithal to do it. Blakemere was good in that respect—its hospitality was a well-oiled routine, and every age and taste was catered for. And of course the taste of young people for food was amply met on this occasion—grossly, wastefully, too richly catered for, so that the poor children of the village on whom it was off loaded the next day were gorging themselves on unaccustomed delicacies for weeks afterward, and making themselves very ill.

"Why are children given plain nursery fare for three hundred and sixty days a year, and disgustingly rich food on birthdays and holidays?" I asked Peter Coverdale as we watched the infant gentry stuffing themselves.

"I always imagined nursery food at Blakemere would be rather grand," said Peter disparagingly. "Everything else is."

All bad times come to an end. Eventually the adult gorging was over, the bride and groom disappeared to various appointed bedrooms and reemerged smartly dressed for going away, on the first leg of their journey to the south of France—a conventional choice, perhaps Uncle Frank's way of suggesting that this was a conventional marriage: one of convenience, mercenary and unromantic. They mingled for a while with the guests, she immensely self-assured, he terribly diminished. He sauntered up awkwardly as I stood watching a cricket game on the lawns from the windows of the Conservatory.

"Well—it's done," he mumbled.

"Yes, it's done," I replied, looking at him. His eyes dropped to the floor and he wandered off.

It was as if the light of my life had been dimmed to a flickering rush. I could bear it no longer. No mere Miss Roxby could stop me. I ran from the Conservatory, along corridors, up the grand staircase, up less grand staircases, along dingier corridors, and finally threw myself on my own bed in my own little room, and sobbed and sobbed, eventually sobbing myself to sleep, only to awaken in the night to sob again.

In my fancy, remembering it now, I form the notion that if I were to go and unboard Blakemere, turn on the switched-off power, go down the dusty corridors again, up the uncarpeted stairs, and find again my little bedroom, I would feel the mattress and it would still be damp from my tears.

CHAPTER SIX

Happy Event

They returned from the honeymoon after six weeks, two weeks earlier than planned. When I heard they were due at Blakemere there was no lifting of the heart for me, though the news intrigued me. I accounted for the change of plan by deciding that he was so bored by her company—and he must have had a great deal of it, even in the midst of what I thought of as the "mad whirl" of the south of France—that he was desperate to return home, dump her at Blakemere, and go about his business.

There was an element of truth in my conjectures, but they were not the whole truth.

When Uncle Frank brought his new bride home (a separate apartment of several rooms had been carved out for them in the South Wing with no difficulty at all), both he and she were different, but subtly so. She was more confident—*still* more so—but she was also complacent, she purred, and I caught her looking round the magnificence of Blakemere's statelier rooms with the same air of calculation I had seen in the eyes of her father.

The difference in Uncle Frank was more difficult to pin down. He was certainly not *jaunty*, as experience has taught me many bridegrooms are: he was casual, flippant, careless of the attentions usual to a new wife. These things I would have expected from his behavior during the engagement period. But there was something else. There were moments when it seemed as if a load had been lifted from his shoulders rather than laid on them. I didn't understand at all.

Within two days of their return there was a visit—a visit made so quietly, almost surreptitiously, that I did not hear of it till some days later—by the foremost medical man in Wentwood, the nearest town of any significance. Almost a week later, from my coign of vantage at the top of the grand staircase to the first floor, I heard a departing visitor say to my grandmother, "And when is the happy event?"

Happy event! I turned and scurried to my room, my cheeks burning, my eyes starting to fill. So *that* union was going to produce *that* result! I would have been infinitely happier if it had produced no result at all—not because I was jealous at being supplanted, but because a barren marriage would have been the only appropriate sort in the circumstances. There was no love, ergo there should be no child.

As I resorted and replaced my ideas, things began to fall into place: the early return from Nice; the new confidence of the bride. Uncle Frank had done what was expected of him and ensured the future of Blakemere and Fearing's Bank.

Provided, of course, it was a boy.

In the next few weeks Uncle Frank fulfilled my predictions by being away from Blakemere and his new wife for long periods. Mary (I never called her Aunt Mary if I could avoid it) did not seem to mind. Quite the contrary, in fact: I think she felt she could consolidate her position at Blakemere best on her own and in her own way. She remained entirely respectful to Grandpapa and Grandmama, but she had decided she could largely ignore my father, and she concentrated her energies on carving out niches for herself where she could be supreme, where no one would dispute her authority. She appointed two maids for herself, she arranged the decoration and equipment of a nursery, she had special meals cooked for herself alone and ate them in her own apartment. She began to visit in the village, to dispense her own charities, attach to herself by moderate largesse or by employment Melbury people whose ties to the family had previously been general rather than particular. Perhaps most newly married women would have done likewise, but, observing her actions, I sensed a specially calculated brand of selfishness.

The servants hated her.

Her own maids less obviously so, but they hated her nonetheless. The only mode she had of treating domestic staff was a coldness veering toward disdain. The old family servants showed their feelings by never embroidering any mention of her name. The mention of any other family member might be embroidered along the lines of: "The salmon mousse is for Lady Fearing—you know how much she loves it." The equivalent for Mary would be: "The salmon mousse is for Mrs. Francis," with silence left after the name both by the speaker and by the person spoken to. If they could have made it even more formal by saying "Mrs. Francis Fearing" without sounding ridiculous in the Fearing household, they would have done.

Uncle Frank, on his rare visits to Blakemere, did not change in his demeanour toward his wife, but he did seem to be increasingly delighted by the prospect of becoming a father. He also made efforts to mend his bridges with me. He did not need to try very hard. My respect for him was dented, but my love hardly at all. This was the period when he taught me tennis (my game has always been rather mannish as a consequence), and occasionally we would have one of our old companionable days fishing on the riverbank.

"You'll have to bring the little one out fishing when I'm not at Blakemere," he said, on one of them. "Which I don't intend to be very much."

"By the time your son is old enough to fish," I said, my eyes on the far bank and the meadows beyond it, "I shouldn't think I shall be much at Blakemere myself."

You notice I didn't use endearments about the approaching baby, though I did suspect that when it arrived I would be unable to resist its charms.

"Aha! And what will you be doing in the big world, little rabbit? Studying life in order to be a writer?"

I giggled. "You promised not to call me that anymore. I've changed my mind about what I want to be."

"Quite right, too. Never set yourself goals too early on."

"I think I'm going to be a wonderful nurse and social reformer like Florence Nightingale."

Uncle Frank let out a great Hrrrmff. "Florence Nightingale these days is nothing but a great hypochondriac and a great nuisance to everyone in government. What she needs is a nurse of the old school, who would either kill her or shake some sense into her. And social reformers, though sometimes admirably useful, tend to be the sort of person that sensible people go miles to avoid."

"That's because most people don't like having their eyes opened to the truth," I said solemnly. "I think you are essentially frivolous, Uncle Frank."

"Of course I am. Would you like me half as much if I wasn't?"

"No."

"Then consider yourself very fortunate that you have been spared a social reformer as your uncle."

We fished on companionably for a while.

"What if the little one is a girl?" I blurted out eventually.

My uncle shrugged. "What if it is? *You* know I love little girls. I'll teach her to fish, as I've taught you, *and* to play tennis."

"The family will want a boy."

His face reddened, and he turned to me almost fiercely.

"The family be damned! God rot them, each and every one. I've delivered my side of the bargain."

Thinking over those words today, I think Uncle Frank was saying that sexual relations with his wife were at an end. At the age of thirteen I knew next to nothing about how babies came into the world. Who in the family did I have to ask? Who would think to take it on themselves to tell me when the right age came? Beatrice had told me only that this was something "between men and women," and that I would be told about it "when the time came." I suspected the time would never come. I suppose I could have asked Uncle Frank, but his marriage, the reasons for it, his reluctance to go through with it, made doing that more, not less difficult.

I did ask Beatrice again on one of my visits to the spruce little cottage on the perimeter of Tillyards, that warm, red-brick old manor house with so many cold-hearted people inside.

"Bea, tell me how babies are made."

Bea was also expecting a happy event. She was sure to know.

"It's something between a man and a woman."

"So you've said. *Tell* me."

She got the usual cagey expression on her face. I knew it well.

"Something a man and a woman do together. . . . It's not for me to tell you. Someone will at the right time."

Oddly enough, I accepted that from her, and was distracted on to a topic that interested me more.

"Bea, was Mary liked when she was Mary Coverdale and lived at Tillyards?"

For answer, Beatrice merely rolled her eyes. She did not need to say any more. Servants always *know*, I said to myself triumphantly. We got on to talking about the approaching lying-in which was to produce her eldest son—the imaginatively named Merlin South (Bea had always loved storybooks with pictures). In later years he was for a time chauffeur at Tillyards, then a commercial traveler, and is now managing a factory producing wireless sets in Bedford—not a magician, by any means, but a solid, sensible man. Anyway, I learned something about the birth of babies from her, even if I learned nothing about procreation.

This knowledge did allow me to make some judgments on the preparations for the lying-in at Blakemere, and to discuss them with Miss Roxby. I told myself that Miss Roxby probably knew as little as I did about lyings-in and how babies were made, but that was not in fact true. She knew plenty about them, and was certainly interested in the approaching "happy" event.

"I think all these preparations are flying in the face of Providence," I said. It was a phrase I was fond of.

"It's hardly flying in the face of Providence to prepare for something that you know is going to happen," she pointed out. I shook my head impatiently.

"I mean the *scale* of the preparations. Dr. Morris from Wentwood is to be in residence here for a week before the poor little thing is due, and our fastest horse is to be in readiness for the coachman to ride to Aylesbury to summon Dr. Petherbridge. How absurd! And the number of midwives, nurses, extra servants that have been hired—as if we didn't have enough already!"

"Perhaps Mrs. Francis insists on them," said Miss Roxby slyly.

"Perhaps she does! It would be in character. But it doesn't alter the absurdity."

"I believe some of the extra servants are already causing problems below stairs," said Miss Roxby. "Incomers usually do."

"Were you ill last night?" I asked.

"Ill? No, why?"

"I heard Robert come from your room."

"I sent for hot milk. I found it difficult to sleep."

My doubts about the preparations were only confirmed in the weeks ahead, for they became more and more grandiose, and Blakemere might more reasonably have been awaiting the birth of an heir to the throne instead of an heir to the banking firm of Fearing's. But Uncle Frank was not party to these preparations. How could he be, when he was hardly ever there? The preparations could be laid to the account of my grandfather and his exaggerated sense of the family's importance. I think I have hinted that my grandmother was much the more intelligent of the two. I suspect she adopted the policy of many women married to stupid (or *limited* would be a fairer estimate) men, and let him have his head in public, hoping to influence him privately, if only in small ways. In the matter of the approaching birth he had his own way entirely, and if the ironic eye might have said he made a great fool of himself, such an eye (and there were not many at Blakemere, apart perhaps from my grandmother, and Uncle Frank) would have made sure his perceptions never were given verbal expression.

Uncle Frank was summoned home by telegram one week before the birth. They should have known him better. Nothing had actually happened, and he knew perfectly well when the baby was expected. He ignored the summons and came down three days later. I saw him greet his wife in Grandmama's sitting room: he could have been an atheist in court kissing the Bible. His jokes about her size were brushed aside, as all jokes were by Mary. She told him the opinions of the doctors, which interested him, then outlined her plans for the future of their son, which interested him not at all. Uncle Frank intended to make all the important decisions about the boy's future himself. And if I knew Uncle Frank, there would be no element of predestination in the plans—no sense that the child was born for one fate and one fate alone. He thought of himself as a free spirit, and his son would be the same.

The labor began two days late. Mary, I was told, had been very impatient with the delay, as if a tradesman had not turned up on time for an appointment. The birth was to take place not in her own bedroom, but in one of the largest bedchambers in the body of the house. Grandpapa had not actually asked the Home Secretary to witness the birth, but if he had thought he would come, he would have done so. I need hardly say I was kept well away from the center of so much drama and expectation.

"What happens when a baby is born?" I asked Miss Roxby, though, as I say, I doubted she knew much more than me.

"It is a time of great pain and suffering for the mother," she said. "Great joy eventually, too, of course."

This last was definitely an afterthought, and one reluctantly brought out. I perceived I was not going to get anything but generalities.

"And how long does it take?"

"It can be quite short, and it can be horribly long."

Again, she seemed to speak with intense feeling.

"It doesn't sound as if you ever want to have a baby."

"I don't. I had an elder sister die in childbirth. There are ways of avoiding it."

It had never occurred to me that childbirth was unavoidable, so I said rather priggishly, "It's a good job *some* people want to have babies, or what would become of the Country?"

"There will always be plenty of women who find their vocation in having babies and bringing up children," said Edith Roxby.

I thought of Beatrice, and nodded.

I became less sure that I was one of them when the labor started.

I was, as I say, well away from the bedroom in question, and was denied my usual freedom to roam. However, I registered the beginning of the birth (the phrase I used to myself) by the sounds of servants scuttling around, and by a series of subtle changes in the routines of the house. That was not long after breakfast. I said nothing to Miss Roxby, but bent low over my schoolbooks. For some reason my cheeks were burning. When the usual time came for a break in lessons, Edith led me down an obscure back staircase and stayed with me as we roamed well away from the house, talking of all sorts of miscellaneous matters that were not really what was on our minds. The servant who brought us our dinner (our main meal was served at about two, this being thought healthy for a child) was flurried, and whispered to Miss Roxby. When she had gone, my governess told me that the birth was difficult and protracted, but it was hoped it would soon be over.

She was remembering her sister, I knew. Mary was not loved, but a death in childbirth strikes chill in the hearts of all women.

But the labor was not soon over. The afternoon wore on, evening came, the sun sank low in the sky. I tried to imagine "great pain and suffering" lasting as long as this, and failed utterly. I had not had a happy childhood, but my physical pains had been few and short.

"How *can* it go on so long?" I asked Miss Roxby, feeling almost sorry for Mary.

"It often does. It's women's lot."

"It won't be *mine*."

At last I sensed, by the house's noises, that it was over. It was as if the whole mountainous structure relaxed. I had no sense of tragedy, of the house having been struck by an unusual disaster. I wondered what would happen to me. Would I just go to bed in the usual way? Surely someone would understand what a child feels about a new baby in the house?

Miraculously someone did. Almost two hours after I had sensed that the house was relaxing, almost rejoicing, Robert, our favorite footman, knocked on the schoolroom door.

"Miss Sarah is to go and see the new baby."

I didn't quite like the way he put it, but there was no question of my refusing to go. I got up and led the way, Miss Roxby behind me, and Robert a short but respectful distance behind her. We went down one flight, then through endless, progressively grander corridors till we came to the immense and gloomy bedroom where I knew the lying-in had taken place. Robert knocked on the door, and Mr. McKay, looking as grand as grand (grander than any Home Secretary could have looked) let us in.

Mary, on the bed, was white, drowsy, but triumphant. Uncle Frank was not by her but beside the cradle, and he looked—how can I analyze it?—pleased with himself, for once not dissatisfied or ashamed over the shoddy bargain he had been forced into, and above all proud of the little bundle in white lying quiet in the ridiculously grand cradle in the center of the room.

"Can I hold him?"

I knew it must be a him. The medical man, immensely portly and pompous, looked dubious, but Uncle Frank said, "Of course," and took up the little bundle tenderly. I held my breath, feeling it would break like a china doll if he dropped it. Then I put out my arms and he put the bundle into them. I looked down into the quiet, sleeping little face and I felt a love so overpowering, so all-embracing for the helpless little thing that I realized I had never felt love before—that my affection for Uncle Frank was the natural feeling I would have for one of the few attractive people in my life, but that this was the real thing—the passion that took hold of you, took over your life, filled every part of your body and mind.

The eyes in my little bundle opened, the face screwed up, and he began to whimper.

CHAPTER SEVEN

Son and Heir

Physically the baby thrived. I was delighted, but a little surprised. Blakemere did not seem to be the sort of place where babies would flourish. A *grand* nursery, for example, seemed a contradiction in terms, yet since the baby had to have a nursery in the body of the house, close to its mother, a grand nursery was what he had. And a *grand* nursery, of course, was what Grandpapa thought appropriate. A large, authoritative woman from Wentwood, Mrs. Nealson, was the nurse in charge, and it was Mrs. Nealson whom I had to propitiate if I wanted to hold my little cousin, tickle him to make him gurgle, dangle things before his eyes, or put things in his chubby little hands. She was, I think, a good woman at bottom, but she was a very fearsome one at top, and for her I was the model little girl which I was for no one else.

It was Mrs. Nealson who noticed first. Cousin Richard (as he was to be christened) was Mary's first child, so though he got what was called his infant succor from her, it was natural she wouldn't remark it. To me a baby was as foreign as a kangaroo would be if one was imported to graze on Blakemere's grassy expanses, so there was no question of my noticing.

I got no whisper of it when Mrs. Nealson first brought the matter out into the open. I think I may have heard of a joint visit to the nursery by Dr. Morris and Dr. Petherbridge, but I thought this was merely routine—high-level routine, certainly, but that would have been in keeping with all Grandpapa's other dealings during the pregnancy and the lying-in.

My uncle Frank was summoned home from Paris, and this time he came.

The news, the awful news, gradually seeped down to me.

Richard was not responding as a baby of six weeks should—not observing, not reacting. In a word—and it was a word that began to be whispered around even below stairs—he was "backward." Worse than that, he was what we today would call retarded. Under their breaths the servants used the word "idiot."

I was never told whether this was due to something either of the doctors had done during the delivery, and I made no inquiries later on when I was in a position to. To what end? And it would have seemed too much like trying to attribute *blame*. How could I want to put blame on anyone for the condition of a boy, a man, who was so much happier and nicer than anyone else at Blakemere?

The medical men came fairly frequently, together or separately, for several weeks after that. I think, like most professional people, they had an aversion to delivering bad news with any brutal suddenness: doing it by dribs and drabs is much more beneficial financially. Certainly Mary was a long time taking the news in: she went on feeding the quiet, plump little bundle, and seemed to think that his condition might be reversed by treatment—an operation, or a course of the waters.

When the truth was revealed to her, her world fell apart. The fact that it was an unlovely world, a piece of self-glorification and self-aggrandisement, did not make its shattering any the less appalling. She continued feeding Richard, but she otherwise preferred not to see him. Any nursing, cradling, cuddling he got came from his father, or from me, or from one of the women paid to take care of him, who felt their importance suddenly diminished. It bound me still more tightly to Uncle Frank that the confirmation that his son was mentally retarded did not shake by one iota the love that he felt for him.

"It's obvious that sooner or later he will have to be put in an institution," I heard Mary say one day to her husband. "Best for him if it's sooner."

She said "him" as if she wanted to say "it." They were on the terrace, and I saw Uncle Frank's face darken, and he strode off without a word down to the meadows.

I think if he could have chosen, Uncle Frank would have been much more at Blakemere from then on. But it was not to be thought of: Blakemere contained his wife, and everything she did from the time of the doctors' final pronouncement jangled his nerves and outraged his feelings of justice and decency. The poor little mite had in effect lost both parents.

"I think Richard should go and live with Bea South for a bit," I said to him, one day after tennis. "That way he would get a bit of love."

He looked at me mystified.

"You remember Beatrice. I used to be always talking about her. She used to be an upper parlormaid here—she married the coachman at Tillyards about the time you married . . . your wife. She gave *me* love when I needed it."

He hesitated, attracted by the idea, yet reluctant.

"I wouldn't want it thought it was in any way like putting him away in an asylum."

"It wouldn't be. It would be just while he is a baby. Babies are often put out to nurse. Bea has a son, too—they would be together, and it might . . . help."

Uncle Frank thought about it, and two days later we rode over together and he broached the possibility to Bea. She would have agreed whatever her feelings were—she was loyal to the Fearings without being starry-eyed about them. What sensible person could be? In fact, she was delighted, as I knew she would be.

Mary, when the idea was put to her, agreed with a shameful alacrity, though she made it clear that to her mind it was merely the prelude to the inevitable institutionalizing of Richard. She was not, at this period, behaving at all wisely. I think the crash of her hopes had unsettled her calculating brain. I imagine she clung to the thought that she was still, in spite of everything, wife to a Fearing and mother to one. She did not realize just how empty such titles could be. She had only to look at my mother to understand that.

I have no doubt she still had hopes of producing another heir.

I think that thought was at the back of everyone's mind. Indeed, it occasionally occurred to me, but I had other and less distasteful things to think about. The arrangements for Richard were first among them, and they involved several visits to Tillyards, which were a great delight. Uncle Frank accompanied me if he was at Blakemere, and he and Bea got on famously. He was less taken with Tom South, her husband.

"Mark my words," he said, as we rode home one day, "she'll have trouble with that one."

"Why do you say that?"

"He's jealous of his own son. Can you imagine a man being that? And with another on the way, it won't get any better."

Mrs. Nealson took her dismissal with good grace, and expressed the wish to be of service in the future. She was probably in some sort of conspiracy. I never saw Uncle Frank's reaction to this remark when it was repeated to him, as it surely was, but I was with him when, in one of the less cumbersome family carriages, and accompanied by Mrs. Nealson, we took Richard over to the cottage on the edge of the Tillyards estate and handed him over to Bea. They took to each other at once, and Richard showed delight in having another baby around him. He was a placid, often listless baby, but he had the capacity to express spontaneous delight that never left him during his short life. As we slipped away, Mrs. Nealson said it was "probably for the best," and we both agreed with her, though for both of us it was only a short-term measure, and it was left to me to make sure that was what it was.

It was no part of Uncle Frank's plan (though it certainly was of Mary's) that Richard should be shunted off to Bea's cottage and forgotten. It was arranged from the start that Bea should bring him over once a fortnight to Blakemere.

"Got to get him used to the monstrous pile," said Uncle Frank. "Poor little beast."

This pleased Bea, because it enabled her to renew friendships with the Blakemere staff formed while she worked here. It pleased me, because I could take charge of him while he was here, especially if Uncle Frank was away. It pleased Mary not at all, and she usually kept to her apartment while he was on his visit, causing much adverse comment below stairs.

It was on one such visit, when Richard was about nine months old, that I overheard a conversation between my grandfather and Uncle Frank. Well, overheard is a genteelism, because I eavesdropped; and conversation is another, because they were having a row. Uncle Frank had wheeled Richard in his magnificent perambulator with the new pneumatic tires—ordered before his birth, and apparently designed with a Brobdingnagian baby in mind—over to a clump of trees just reaching maturity at the brow of the slope leading down to the river. There they had paused, and unseen by Uncle Frank (he would have sped off, I felt sure, if he had noticed), Grandpapa came purposefully over from the terrace. I was reading in the summer sun some way away, but the moment they became engaged in conversation I stood up and slipped silently over till I could hide behind the trunk of a reasonably sturdy oak. Nothing at Blakemere, remember, was actually old. The conversation was already becoming warm in tone. I heard my grandfather first.

"Of course I wouldn't want to come between husband and wife."

"There's nothing to come between."

Grandfather tugged at his mustaches.

"You know what I mean. I would rather we could leave you to yourselves to sort out your difficulties."

Uncle Frank shrugged. "There are no difficulties. We understand each other perfectly."

"You know very well that is not the case. In fact, everyone in the house knows that relations between you are . . . not on a normal footing."

"I should have thought they were pretty much the same footing as those of my brother Claudius and his wife."

"Don't be ridiculous!" exploded my grandfather, almost tugging his mustaches off in his exasperation. "You know there is no question of Claud and Harriet providing Blakemere with an heir."

"I don't see what that has to do with anything."

"It has everything to do with everything. Your debts were paid, an allowance was given you for life, and in return you were to marry and provide Blakemere with an heir."

"How admirably you express our business arrangement, Papa," Uncle Frank said, with that irony which must have been so irritating. "It sounds like one in the Old Testament between God and a mere mortal. But you can't play God, Father. You can't order events just to suit your own plans. I've fulfilled my side of the bargain." He pointed to the pram. "There's your heir to Blakemere."

And, choking with rage, he set off with Richard down the hill to the river. Grandpapa was by now red with a combination of embarrassment and anger. He watched father and son for a moment, fuming, then turned and stumped back to the house. I kept myself on the furthest side of the oak, away from him, then, as he disappeared into the distance, I walked through the clump of trees to watch Uncle Frank.

Miss Roxby and I were embarking on the novels of Sir Walter Scott and were reading *The Bride of Lammermoor* (the first of innumerable disappointments). Uncle Frank's words reminded me of the story it was based on, and the words of poor mad Janet Dalrymple, as retailed in the Introduction, after she had stabbed the husband she had been forced to marry: "Tak up your bonny bridegroom." I was sure Uncle Frank intended no cruelty about the poor son he loved so much. But the sight of his moon face in the magnificent baby carriage must have pointed up with poignant clarity the overreaching blasphemy of my grandfather in trying to organize human events to suit his grand plan for the Fearing family and its bank. Johnson called it the vanity of human wishes. Something in Uncle Frank's stance as he wheeled the perambulator toward the tranquility of the river suggested that he was hating himself for using his son to score a debating point off his father. He was quiet for several days after that, and very thoughtful.

Not that this brought him peace. I overheard, and Miss Roxby overheard, and even Bea on her fortnightly visits to Blakemere overheard various members of the family making niggling remarks to him on the subject of the need for a new heir. Aunt Jane's was the most indirect and genteel, as befitted her status as a maiden sister.

"We all do hope you and dear Mary will be a family again soon," she said to him one day in the library when he was searching for a book to assuage his boredom. He merely grunted. Grandmama, I regret to say (for I respected her) was more trenchant.

"It's time you did your duty by Blakemere and did your duty as a husband," she said. She had for the moment taken on her husband's order of priorities, I fear. Uncle Frank did not even honor this with a grunt. Any respect he had once had for his parents vanished at the time of his forced marriage.

I am approaching the crucial event of my girlhood, the climax of this botched attempt to manipulate the strongest and most private human feeling. I shall find the telling difficult, for at the time I knew so little and understood even less. I walked yesterday, with my dogs Lizzie and Ernie bounding beside me, to the boarded-up blankness of Blakemere, thinking not of my duties at the present time, but of those long-ago days in 1893.

It was almost funny, in these days of austerity, to look on the bloated facades of Blakemere. What on earth could be done with it today—what could the house *be*? It was not suitable for anything—and certainly not for a house. Even if Victorian architecture were to come back into fashion, Blakemere was only notable for magnificence. My great-grandfather and grandfather stinted on nothing except the architect. Taste and style had they none, and he had delivered them a building that was suitably tasteless and styleless.

But in the context of the house's heyday the magnificence was all. And thinking of my uncle's marriage, its distastefulness to himself, I had to admit that many royal marriages at the time were contracted on a similar bases. Wasn't May of Teck at around this time passed from one dead brother to the next living one like a parcel because she so obviously was cut out to make a formidable Queen (she had not then developed those kleptomaniac tendencies that today make her the terror of antique shop and stately home owners)? The magnificence of Blakemere made the Fearings see themselves as semi-royal, and behave accordingly.

"The Bank" everyone used to say in the hushed, reverent tones that royalty might use when they talked of "The Country." Blakemere was named in plump, proprietorial fashion, as royalty might name the finest of its palaces. My grandfather, pacing the spacious rooms, corridors, and staircases of Blakemere, thought of himself as a king—and no tinpot or parvenu king of a Balkan state, either, but the genuine royal article.

That was one factor in the approaching combustion. The other was the unbridgeable gap between my grandparents' insistence that Uncle Frank keep his side of the bargain, and Uncle Frank's conviction that he already had.

CHAPTER EIGHT

ERUPTION

The day before the eruption of the family volcano that was to change my whole life, and the lives of many of the other inmates of Blakemere, Uncle Frank arrived in the early evening. He went straight to his old bedroom. There was no longer any pretense of marital relations between him and Mary, and indeed even when they returned from honeymoon they had had separate bedrooms in their apartment. Now, apparently, he could not bear even to be so close to her. This much I had learned from eavesdropping in the servants' hall. Later on, Uncle Frank dined with the family. He was, I was told, rather morose, so I made no moves in his direction but rather waited on him to initiate some. At breakfast time there was a note from him, brought by Robert, begging a morning off lessons for me so that we could go over and see Richard and Bea.

So he was not morose with me. I changed my dress, got into my coat, and we set off with delight.

Unbeknownst to me things happened while we were away. People posted "o'er land and ocean without rest." A footman on horseback took the same route as us to Tillyards with an important message. Telegrams were sent elsewhere, summoning interested parties. Aunt Jane was taken in one of the house's lesser carriages toward Wentwood, where she had a serious talk with Aunt Sarah. Relations between the two were perfectly friendly but not warm. This was probably due to Aunt Sarah's "oddity" (anything not perfectly orthodox in opinions and behavior was counted odd, and atheism and an independent life certainly qualified as not perfectly orthodox, especially in a woman). Sarah's "oddity" probably also accounted for the fact that Aunt Jane's mission was unsuccessful: she declined to be one of the party which was massing to bring Uncle Frank into line.

We only became aware of this activity when we returned to Blakemere after a happy morning with Richard and with Bea's little son Merlin. I had looked for any sign that contact with the assertive, lively boy was acting as a tonic to Richard's listless brain, and in my depths of love for the boy I thought I saw some. Uncle Frank agreed, whether from conviction or to keep my spirits up I do not know. It was as we drove up to the Grand Entrance to Blakemere that he said, "Uh huh. Something's up."

We were still half a mile away, and I could not see who was getting out of the carriage that was drawn up in the center of that endless facade of sub-medieval castle.

"It's Anselm," explained Uncle Frank. "Anselm and Margaret. Anselm the Unreliable and Margaret the Unremarkable."

It was very naughty of Uncle Frank to speak of our relatives in this way, and I was delighted. Anselm Fearing was head of the younger branch of the Fearing family, son of Grandpapa's younger brother. He was also father to Digby Fearing, who is currently running Fearing's bank in my absence on more important matters, and running it very capably. It always amazes me how children can turn out so totally different from any of their parents or even grandparents. I have never had a moment of doubt about Digby's probity, yet there hung about his father (and even at twelve I could sense it) an air of unreliability, of being only as honest as staying within the law required, of having an eye for an easy profit and a sharp deal.

He was, of course, the father of that brood of male Fearings who were always spoken of as a sort of last resort, if the male Fearings descended from male Fearings descended from my grandfather should fail, and if I (as everyone I think expected) should decline the honor of becoming the head of the family. The moment Uncle Frank mentioned his name I realized that the family was assembling to put the maximum possible pressure on my uncle to patch up his marriage and (to put the matter in the sort of language that was being used at the time) to "try again." It puzzled me, this arrival of Cousin Anselm, because it was not in his interest, or that of his sons, that Frank should try again, and I wondered why he should join the forces arraigned against him. With hindsight, and greater knowledge of the man and his ways, I suspect that he was offered a substantial inducement to do so. He would be bound to prefer goodies then and there, and for him, over goodies in the future for his sons. Cousin Margaret was a doting mother who would want only the best for her children, but hers was not a voice that was ever listened to.

"So the forces of attack are massing," said Uncle Frank in an odd voice. He thought about it, then rubbed his hands. "I rather think I am going to enjoy this."

"Poor Frank!" I think now, and my eyes still fill with tears.

He did not speak again till we drew up at the Entrance, but then he turned to me and spoke earnestly.

"If I have to break with the family," he said, "see to it that Richard has all the love you can give him."

I nodded my promise—the promise that was to dominate my life for the next twenty-five years and more. But at the time the only thing I could think about was the dreadful gap that would be left in my life if Uncle Frank were to leave Blakemere forever. When we got inside, I ran to my room to have a brief sob. Then I put a brave face on it and went to have my dinner with Miss Roxby.

In the course of the afternoon Cousin Margaret came to the schoolroom and sat in on a history lesson. I suppose she could not think of anything else to do. She was a dumpy, comfortable soul who let her life revolve around children. She stayed on to talk to Miss Roxby during my break. I went out on to the autumnal meadows, where the trees were starting to be tinged with yellow and brown. From there I watched Cousin Anselm walking up and down the terrace with a woman whose bonnet shielded her face. Anselm had the sort of droopy mustache that straggles down to the chin—a sort of mustache I always associate with fraudsters and murderers. It did nothing for his features: his weak mouth, insignificant nose, and wandering eyes. At one point they turned to look at the river, and I realized the woman was Aunt Clare. I wondered what purpose her summoning could serve, beyond that of swelling the numbers. Perhaps it was thought that her romantic temperament, if it had survived fifteen years of marriage to a bad artist, would bring forth an eloquent defense of marriage, and a moving plea to Uncle Frank to make one last effort to right his foundering matrimonial barque.

I was, of course, free of the whole house (so long as my legs would stand the marathon distances involved), and I went down to the kitchens to observe preparations. They were nothing special so far as I could see.

"Just an ordinary family dinner," confirmed Mr. McKay, and Mrs. Needham nodded.

An ordinary Fearing dinner would of course feed a small village for a month on 1946 rations, but I took the point. Dinner was not what all this was about. Later on, when the house's thousand clocks told me the family would have finished sherry and gone in to eat, I went down and lurked outside the Green Dining Room, where the family ate when they were on their own, much less grand than the splendid banqueting hall used for honored guests such as Mr. Gladstone. A small staff was serving the fish course. Conversation was fairly general, but muted and stilted. Sir Thomas Coverdale's goatee beard wiggled and he talked in hushed tones to Grandmama, while his wife (a showy woman, but nicer in my eyes) was finding it fairly hard going with Grandpapa. My father looked as if he were a thousand miles away. Uncle Frank stared at his baked cod as if it were something on a mortuary slab. Mary was sitting at the other end of the table, her rosebud mouth pursed, her eyes troubled and discontented. It was as if she, one of the central figures, had resigned herself to defeat before the battle had even started.

An idea occurred to me. If the concerted attack on Uncle Frank was not to occur at dinner, it must be scheduled for later—probably over coffee and liqueurs in the sitting room. I walked demurely down the corridor, then, when I was out of sight, sped to the room in question—the dark crimson, high, horribly overfurnished room that the family used for what passed for every day. Coffee cups were already set out, also dishes with chocolates and tiny cakes, and several large bowls of fruit, more and less exotic, with plates and knives beside them. The blue velvet curtains were already drawn. I ran over to one of the windows, got behind the curtains, and opened it—a modest slit of an opening but sufficient for my purposes, I thought. Then I went upstairs, kissed Miss Roxby good night, and went to my room, ostensibly to go to bed.

An hour would see them through dinner, I calculated. I sat on my bed, not sure what to do. I sometimes read for a while when I went to bed, if I had anything exciting under way (*Jane Eyre*, for example, or *Oliver Twist*), but mostly I went straight to sleep. I knew I wouldn't be able to settle to reading that night, and feared that if I tried I would probably fall asleep. There were soft footsteps in the corridor and I wondered who it was: our part of the house was mostly deserted at night. I thought about the approaching confrontation and decided that the family would almost certainly lose: Uncle Frank having it already in mind to break with the Fearings suggested that, as did his invincible distaste for the wife they had forced on him. The Fearing clan, I concluded, had very few good cards in their hands. Soon after eight, darkness having fallen, I put on my coat, scuttled along back corridor after back corridor, then down an obscure staircase and to a back door that gave on to the terrace. The night air came as some relief to hectic, troubled thinking.

The window in the sitting room that I had opened looked out over the croquet lawn and the rose gardens nearby. I had no fear for myself in the surrounding vastness of the Blakemere estates, only fear for Uncle Frank—or rather the fear of losing him. I recognize now that my concern was essentially selfish, as children's usually are. I approached silently, or as silently as was possible over graveled paths. I heard a voice as I was still some way away.

"Let's get it over with."

It was my father's voice, the first and only time he contributed.

"Agreed" came Uncle Frank's voice.

"If I may presume, as a relative outsider—" This was the voice of Sir Thomas Coverdale, one I knew less well, but unmistakable. "An *in*terested outsider, of course, but one who has not been involved in any wrangling or recriminations—"

"You have been the model in-law" came Uncle Frank's ironic tones. "You have kept out of it."

"Nevertheless, the difficulties of the marriage have distressed Mary's mother and me, because of course she has talked all the problems over—"

"The last thing I'd try to do is to stop her having a heart-to-heart. If such is possible."

"Frank!" said my grandmother commandingly. I was now just beside the window, and though the heavy velvet curtains prevented my seeing anything, I could imagine her look.

"The point I would make," resumed Sir Thomas, "is that marriages where the heart is not . . . not *initially* engaged, if I may put it so, are not uncommon among people such as ourselves . . . gentlefolk with a position to maintain locally and nationally, and that such marriages quite often go through a crisis early on. But a modus vivendi is almost always found. Where there's a will . . . It is Lady Coverdale's and my devout wish that such may be the outcome in this marriage, on which so much rests."

He sounded like the Archbishop of Canterbury.

"You are ignoring the fact," said Uncle Frank, his voice even and unemotional, "that such marriages are willingly undertaken, with both parties clear in their minds what they are doing: making an alliance, ensuring the family's continuance and stability, extending its influence or boundaries."

"Well?"

"Mine was not willingly undertaken. It was entered into as a result of strong and continuous pressure from my family."

"You condemn yourself by saying that."

"I am aware of the fact."

That was the end of Sir Thomas Coverdale's attempts at mediation. The next voice to emerge through the thick velvet was, surprisingly, that of Aunt Jane.

"But my dear Frank," she said, her voice unusually sweet, "remember that love may come, bloom, after marriage, and with the coming of little ones."

"That, my dear Jane, is a view of marriage that comes from reading rather than observation. Look at Claud and Harriet."

"I was aware" came his wife's clear, passionless tones "that Francis did not love me—not in the usual sense."

"Not in any sense. I made that clear."

"What you did not make clear was that you had no intention of trying to make the marriage work."

"That was not the case—then. Though I did have the gravest doubts as to whether it could."

"Then you should never have gone through with it."

Uncle Frank's tone was now totally serious.

"Again—the blame, the criticism, is all on me. I accept that. We entered into a contract that was doomed before it was signed and sealed. I should have recognized that, and set sail for Timbuktu rather than let you enter into it."

"But my dear Frank"—it was Cousin Anselm—"all of us here want to see the marriage work. Margaret and I, though it may seem not to be in our best interests, are desperate to see it back on a firm and happy footing."

"Hmmm."

"Might it not be that, away from the family, in another environment, say on a cruise, maybe to India, or the Cape, that you could on your own sort out a modus vivendi?"

In the darkness I could just imagine his face when he said this. Cousin Anselm was what we today would call smarmy.

"Tried that. Didn't work," said Uncle Frank, with a return to more satirical tones. "Too much of each other just shows us how hopeless it is."

"Not *us*," said Mary.

"Me."

"The truth of the matter is," came the impatient tones of my grandfather, "that the boy made no effort to fulfill his side of the agreement."

I think all this talk of love, of relationships, was inimical to Grandpapa. Contracts, bargains, agreements were more in his line.

"I made every effort to fulfill my side of the agreement, and did so," Uncle Frank said now.

"Then how does it happen that the marriage has come to the sorry state it is now in? Husband and wife separate in the same house. It's unnatural."

"No, it was the marriage itself that was unnatural."

"You are an unmanly cad to describe it so in the presence of your wife."

"Mary knows my feelings. She had no illusions."

His wife's voice rang out.

"I have feelings! Do you think you don't cruelly hurt me when you talk about our marriage like this in front of people?"

"I thought it was precisely to talk about our marriage that this whole confabulation was set up."

"My feelings have never been thought about, not from the very first. You say *you* were pressured into the marriage. But a marriage is a union of two persons. What about me? What about what *I* was led to expect? The position I would occupy? Is it any wonder I'm dissatisfied with what I actually got?"

"No. No wonder at all. So let's end it."

"Think, Frank dear" came the voice of Aunt Clare "how children may alter things, as Jane has said. They would bring you together."

"We have a child. He has driven us further apart."

"How can you compare that . . . that child with the children we might have?" demanded Mary. She was getting on to dangerous ground, but seemed totally reckless.

"How can I? Because I love him."

"You don't love him. You can't. Nobody could. You pretend to love him to annoy *me*, to make people think I am an unnatural mother."

"I don't care in the slightest how people think of you. I love Richard. I have an idea that when he grows up he will be a better person than any of us."

"That's just silly fantasy" came Mary's contemptuous voice.

"Better than us," insisted Uncle Frank. "Because some of the things that make us what we are won't develop in him: greed, jealousy, love of status and position."

"They won't develop in him because he is an idiot."

There was a second of silence, then Uncle Frank hissed, "Don't use that word!"

"He's a cretin, then."

Another silence, then a carefully controlled Frank seemed to turn on the whole assembly around him.

"All right. He's a cretin. Shall I tell you why he is a cretin? Either it's because my family insisted on using an expensive nincompoop at the birth, or else it's because Nature, having created generation after generation of covetous, pushing individuals—greedy gentry, greedy bankers, it makes no great difference—finally said: 'We've got to strike a balance. We've got to show that human beings can be something else, too.' And so it gave us Richard. A wonderful gift."

Mary's voice was hard and ungiving as rock.

"You're talking fantasy. He's only a baby. And when he grows up he will be the mock of the neighborhood."

"Not if I have anything to do with it."

"A rich idiot. Pointed at by everyone." The venom in her voice was palpable even outside in the chill night air. She hated the son who had been born to her, perhaps because she regarded his birth as personal shame.

"You really enjoy saying things like that, don't you? Idiot, cretin. You cold, unfeeling bitch!"

"Frank!" It was Grandmama's voice again.

"I enjoy the truth," said Mary, her voice rising higher. "He'll be a moron, and he'll have to be shut in an asylum."

"Never!"

"Yes, he will. He'll be put away."

"Monster!"

"In a sensible society he'd be put down."

There was a moment's silence. *Some*thing—I had no idea what—was happening.

"You—"

"Frank!"

I heard a scuffle, a great cry from my uncle Frank, several bodies colliding, a punch, a heavy fall. I turned from the window and ran, ran, ran away across the lawn, terrified at the thought of my family fighting, terrified at the thought of father against son, of brother against brother. Who had punched him? What had Frank's terrible cry been caused by? I found the door to the obscure back staircase, and had regained my wits enough to steal in and creep up it, then along the dark, pokey corridors. But as I was turning into my own corridor I held back. A door had opened.

I withdrew round the corner, and waited a moment. Then I poked my head cautiously round and took a look. The footman Robert was emerging from Miss Roxby's bedroom. He looked around him furtively, then stole away from me toward the body of the house. As he turned the corner he squared his shoulders, began to walk more confidently, then disappeared from my view.

Shaken to the heart, I pressed my hot cheeks against the cold stone wall. It was as if my whole world had been violently reversed—first my family world, then my schoolroom world. I stayed like that for what seemed an age. Then I swallowed hard and hared silently along the corridor to my bedroom. Once there I locked the door behind me. I needed very much to be alone. This time I didn't cry, but sat long on my bed, thinking about what I had heard from the sitting room, what I had seen in the corridor outside. Shock, bewilderment, revulsion were succeeded by numbness. Slowly, reluctantly, I took off my clothes, put on my nightdress, and went to bed. Eventually, hours later, I went to sleep.

That night I dreamed a strange dream. I dreamed I woke up in the middle of the night, disturbed by the happenings of the evening, or perhaps by the muffled sound of voices. I lay for a minute or two, mulling over the horror of fighting in the family, of violence against Uncle Frank. Then I was sure I heard a male voice.

I got up quietly and went over to the window. Outside the expanses of Blakemere's park and meadowlands stretched darkly away into the distance, and clouds were sweeping across what moon there was visible. But there was one little patch of light, way below me, and to my left. One of the obscure back entrances to Blakemere was open, and a man with a lantern was standing just outside it. I recognized the shoulders and head of Joe Mossman, one of the gardeners, father to one of my early playmates. He bent down, and seemed to be propping open the door with a slab of stone. I shivered in the night cold, and began twisting the scrap of ribbon that held back my hair. I was nervous with foreboding.

Joe disappeared inside for a moment, but then more light appeared—lanterns, from just inside the house. Then slowly, carefully, I saw another man emerge, and as he moved forward—it was Robert again—I saw he was holding his lantern with difficulty, by its little bow of a handle, because most of his hand was taken up by a pole, and so was his other hand. I saw with horror that he was holding one end of a stretcher, and as he moved forward I saw it contained a long shape, wrapped in some dark stuff that could have been carpeting, and that the other end of the stretcher was held by Joe. And when they had fully emerged and had begun their progress across the terrace, I saw that they were followed by old Ben Burke, one of the family's pensioners from over Wentwood way, and that he was carrying spades.

I let out a squeak of horror and then put my hand to my mouth when I saw that he in his turn was followed by a dark shape in a tall hat, who turned and closed the door behind him. In the gloom I could see almost nothing. I twisted my ribbon, and as the procession, speeding up now, began to cross the meadow toward the little wood on the other side of the river known as Foley's Wood, the ribbon snapped as I thought I recognized the walk of the dark figure who had now gone to the head of the group.

I thought it was my father's walk.

I watched till there was nothing more to see. Then, in my dream, I went back to bed, and finally to sleep. In the morning when I woke I found my hair untidy round my face. I got up and went to the window, and there on the window ledge was a piece of broken ribbon.

CHAPTER NINE

CONSEQUENCES

I was very quiet the next day.

Partly this was because I was upset about what I had overheard the previous evening—upset and uncertain. I was even more upset over what I had seen—*if* I had seen it. On thinking it over it seemed to me that the snapped ribbon proved little. In any case, I knew very well that if I told anybody what I had seen, or thought I had seen, they would have said "You've been dreaming." Even Miss Roxby would have said that. And such a dismissal of my testimony would have been entirely plausible.

Even now I do not *know* that I saw it.

In any case, who could I tell who was a power of any kind in the household? Miss Roxby or someone in the servants' hall would have been the best I could come up with, and I knew what their response would be.

If Miss Roxby noticed my quietness the next day, she did not comment on it. She was very good like that: sympathetic to my moods, but not demonstratively so. We went about our daily round as usual, and of course I did not ask her about Robert the footman.

But a screaming imperative was gaining force within me: I had to know about Uncle Frank. In any case, Miss Roxby was not the obvious person to ask about that, being cut off for much of the time from the body of the house. Failing members of my own family—or, rather, my heart failing at the thought of asking Aunt Jane or my father—I finally decided to ask my friends in the below-stairs part of the house.

"I haven't seen Uncle Frank today," I said to Mrs. Needham, in the afternoon, when preparations for dinner were under way in the kitchens.

"Oh?"

"Is he still in the house?"

"I couldn't say I'm sure. Nobody ever tells me how many there will be for dinner, if it's just a family dinner."

"Well, I know *that*. The waste in this family is shocking." I turned to Mr. McKay, who was pottering around in his intensely dignified way. "Do you know if Uncle Frank is still at Blakemere, Mr. McKay?"

"Ah . . . I *think* not. I rather think he left the house either last night, or very early this morning."

"You must know if his bed had been slept in."

A silly comment. Mr. McKay drew himself up.

"On the contrary, that is not something that comes within my sphere of inquiry. . . . You are getting rather old, Miss Sarah, for coming into the kitchen—or below stairs generally."

"I didn't know there was an age limit," I said, with some of my old pertness.

"A *child* may go anywhere, but a young lady generally keeps herself to her own part of the house. Lady Fearing herself seldom or never comes here—only at Christmas, in fact, to thank the staff for their work over the years, and to distribute gifts."

"It's nice of her to distribute gifts," I said, "but I can't see why she celebrates Christmas at all. Jews don't believe in Christ."

This was in no way pejorative, merely a showing off of a recently acquired piece of knowledge. I knew perfectly well that Grandmama was a Christian. I was not, in fact, diverted from my inquiries, and I meditated who else I might ask. Mrs. Merton, the head housekeeper, was so fantastically discreet and remote that she was out of the question, but I thought I might ask one of the maids. I meandered through the baronial wastelands of the Blakemere servants' hall and kitchens until I spotted Bertha, about some arduous but useless task in a corner. Bertha was sweet and not too bright, which was ideal.

"Bertha, is Uncle Frank still at Blakemere?"

"Oh, no, Miss Sarah Jane—"

"Sarah."

"Miss Sarah. I can't get used to these changes, Miss Sarah J—"

"Uncle Frank."

"He's left."

She said it with no prevarication or embarrassment. But of course if something had happened to Uncle Frank, someone like Bertha would be the last to know.

"Did he go last night or this morning?"

"Last night, I think. His bed wasn't slept in, and all his things are gone. I expect he's gone to London."

It seemed politic to agree.

"I expect he has."

"Powerful fond of London Mr. Frank is, for all he's a married man now."

This was said with what for Bertha passed for cunning.

"Many men find the attractions of London increase after they are married," I said. I think I had been reading Oscar Wilde.

Mention of his "things" made me regret that Uncle Frank had no valet, and used none of the Blakemere servants in lieu of one when he was at home. But her words did suggest to me a course of action I might have followed earlier. Uncle Frank's rooms, his bachelor rooms, were perfectly well known to me, both from visits there while he was at Blakemere, when I was fascinated by their exclusively masculine feel and smell, and from more surreptitious poppings in when he was away, when I was looking for signs that he was expected.

Of course none of the rooms or suites of rooms at Blakemere were kept locked. They might be locked on occasion from inside, for example by people engaged in a blazing row, though not necessarily even then. The desire for privacy is middle class, and we were determinedly no longer middle class. The fact that Uncle Frank had left Blakemere meant that, once the room was done, there was unlikely to be a servant in its vicinity.

It was the second morning after the night of the furious row that, in a break between lessons, I betook myself on the long walk to Uncle Frank's rooms and—my heart thumping, not with fear but with dread of making an unwanted discovery—pushed open the door.

Nothing.

No signs of Uncle Frank at all—not a remnant of his occupancy. The rooms were shiny clean, bare and anonymous. It might have been a luxury suite in a first-class hotel. All the things that Uncle Frank would normally leave here—binoculars, fishing tackle, old overcoats, bottles of his favorite tipples—had been removed. It was almost spiteful in its comprehensiveness. As I stood there I imagined it being done with a sadistic relish: Francis Fearing, it seemed to say, belonged to the house's past; he had no place in the house's future.

I told Miss Roxby what I had discovered later the same day. She received my news without comment; she had these fits of being the faithful, discreet servant of the Fearings. A governess—any servant—had often to act against her own nature.

"It's not fair!" I said passionately. "We lose Uncle Frank forever, and we keep Mary who is not one of us at all!"

"I believe Mrs. Francis has left Blakemere," she said quietly.

That stopped me in my tracks.

"That will please everyone in the servants' hall," I said at last. "And practically everyone above stairs as well."

Miss Roxby said nothing. How I would love to have gone on to talk about the visitor to her room on the fateful night! But I had already trespassed on doubtful ground, on that border territory between the acceptable and the forbidden, and in fact it was many years before that matter could be discussed between us.

But if Miss Roxby was being the loyal servant of popular fiction (a role that did not sit easily on her), with whom could I discuss the fate of Uncle Frank? The memory of that blazing row, of those men in the night, above all of that shape on the stretcher, did not become less vivid as the days passed. It was impossible to imagine discussing Uncle Frank's fate with either of my grandparents, or indeed Aunt

Jane, who still talked to me as if I were in the nursery. With my mother I never had anything that could be called conversation, and indeed I very much doubted if she knew what had happened on the night in question. That left my father.

My father had taken up golf. I spied him from the Library one afternoon a fortnight or so after Uncle Frank's disappearance practicing his putting shots on the croquet lawn. Later he would have his own nine-hole course in the Blakemere grounds, involving more enormous shiftings of earth and creations of artificial hills and woody clumps. How the Fearings did love to improve on Nature's plans! It is now a wilderness, and people wandering there must think that is how that corner of Buckinghamshire has been since the beginnings of time.

On an impulse—thinking it odd I hadn't done this before—I went outside through the obscure door below my bedroom and a little to the left. Once outside I looked around. At the edge of a nearby flower bed there was a heavy stone, such as might be used for propping open a door. I gulped. One more little piece in place. Then I went over toward the croquet lawn and sat on a little wall, watching my father. He made few efforts to talk to me if I did not put myself in his way, but when I did I pricked his conscience. Eventually, as I knew he would, he interrupted his putting and came over, rubbing his hands.

"Capital game," he said. "Absolutely capital. You must take it up. Women can play golf, you know."

"I know."

"Mary, Queen of Scots, for example. She played the game when it was in its infancy."

"I wonder how she found the time," I meditated, genuinely interested in the question. I think I imagined her as fully occupied with love affairs and murderous plots. My father failed to understand my meaning. Uncle Frank would have caught the drift of my thoughts immediately. Papa just stood there rather awkwardly.

"Perhaps you could teach me," I said, to help him out of his embarrassment. "Now that I don't have Uncle Frank to teach me games and things."

He nodded, seemingly pleased.

"Yes, that's a good idea. I know that you and I—"

"Where has Uncle Frank *gone?*" I interrupted him to ask, at least partly to spare shame-making personal stuff.

"Well, I think—Frank has gone to Australia."

"Is he on another expedition? Is he going to cross the Great Australian Desert?"

He rubbed his chin. "Well, not that I know of, but I suppose knowing Frank he might—yes, it would be like him."

"Why else would he go to Australia?"

"I think he aims to stay there quite a while."

"You mean *settle?*"

"Well, yes. I believe that is his intention."

I digested this slowly. I did not believe it was true, but I was careful how I should react.

"He was driven to it," I said at last, passionately. "He should never have been forced to marry."

"He wasn't exactly forced . . . But I think you're right. It was never something I approved of."

"I know." My father was preoccupied, otherwise he might have wondered how I knew.

"Frank and I were never close," he mused, "but I always *liked* him."

"You couldn't not like Uncle Frank."

"No . . . I bitterly regret what happened. They were mismatched from the start. Mary was wronged as much as Frank. I know all about mismatching, about marriages that should never have taken place. But no one put pressure on your mother and me. We were quite willing. And things weren't too bad until . . ."

"Until I came along and was a girl, and she was told she couldn't have any more," I supplied.

"Something like that. You're old enough to understand now."

"Oh, I've always known *that.* So won't Uncle Frank ever come back to this country? Come back here?"

"I shouldn't think so."

"But that's disgusting!" I cried, trying to be my younger, more innocent self. "He belongs here."

My father shook his head.

"I don't think that's true, Sarah Jane. He never belonged here."

And smiling sadly he went back to his putting. It seemed to me that my father was right, and that it was an unusually perceptive remark. Frank had never belonged here. Not at Blakemere, not in nineteenth-century England. I wondered whether Papa had been forced by recent events to think long and seriously about Uncle Frank. I only realized later that where I had said "belongs" he had said "belonged." Even when I realized it, I couldn't quite decide on its significance: he might have been drawing a line not under Uncle Frank's life, but merely under his life at Blakemere.

I watched my father practicing his finishing putts for a few minutes more, then wandered off into the slope beyond the croquet lawn. It was only when I saw him go off toward the house that I directed my feet toward the little wood—the direction I had seen the men walk with the stretcher on the night of Uncle Frank's disappearance. I did not find that day what I was looking for—looking for, yet dreading to find. It was only three visits later, when I had educated myself to spot signs of disturbance, that I found it. It was covered with leaves, branches, and bracken, yet they did not look like the natural ground cover of woodland, such as surrounded them on each side. They were easy to pull away.

Underneath the ground had been dug, and later the earth replaced. The hole had been about six feet by two feet. I gazed at it, then started to cry. After a minute or two I feverishly pulled the bracken and branches back across the bare earth. Then I ran from the place as if pursued, down to the river. It was hours before I went into the house again.

I have never been back to that little wood. I lived at Blakemere all those years until the Second World War, apart from three years at Cambridge, yet in all that time I never went back. If that seems strange, remember that the Blakemere estate is very large—is, indeed, enormous. If I was ever tempted when I was lady of the house to put some kind of memorial there, I restrained the temptation: I am not religious, and in any case I doubted whether I would be able to find the place again. And the memorial would have had to remain blank. Uncle Frank's gravestone was in my heart. Whether he was remembered in anyone else's heart I never knew. Nobody mentioned him, except occasionally the servants—and then, as often as not, only because I was questioning them about him.

I realized soon after this that Grandpapa was failing. Not so much losing his mental powers as physically dying slowly. It was visible in his face, his stance, his grip on what was going on around him—not that he *couldn't* be alert to what was happening, but that he no longer wanted to be. He was still fiercely independent, but he had to assert his independence against the general desire of those around him to minister to his growing weakness, relieve him of all possible cares and duties. I have seen in dogs a similar phenomenon: the loss of any desire to go on living. With them the cause is often a build up of physical ailments, allied to a sense that they've done everything, seen everything, smelled everything, many times.

Grandfather's loss of the will to live I associate with the events of Uncle Frank's last night at Blakemere.

I watched his decline over the two years or so following that night: his increasing difficulty in walking, his use of the bath chair, his needing help even with cutting up his food. And eventually, in the last months, his confinement to his own rooms, with Robert as attendant.

Before that happened, I had one conversation with him that remains in my mind. It was a warm summer's day, and he had been left in his chair on the terrace. His old face was as baggy and blotchy now as Mr. Gladstone's had been ten years earlier, and his body was very much less active. I was playing with Richard, who was on one of his fortnightly visits, where the meadow begins, just down from the terrace. When I first noticed Grandpapa he was looking into the distance, vacantly, but as I came up the steps to talk to him some little signs of life came into his eyes.

"It's a curse, old age, Sarah Jane," he said.

I considerately refrained from correcting his version of my name.

"I can see it is, Grandpapa."

"That's obvious, is it? Well, I suppose if you see an old man in a bath chair with nothing to occupy his mind, it must be pretty clear what an abomination old age is."

"If you ever want me to read to you, Grandpapa—"

"Read? What use is reading now? You read to store up information for the future. I have no future, more's the pity."

"I read for enjoyment, Gra—"

He interrupted me angrily.

"That sort of reading is nothing more than time-wasting. . . . You know, I used to worry about the future. Not anymore. The future will have to take care of itself." He looked at me hard. "Maybe you're the future, Sarah Jane."

"I don't *want* to be, but I suppose if there's only me . . . Grandpapa, has anybody heard from Uncle Frank in Australia?"

"No! And no one's likely to, or wants to!" His eyes looked fiercely at me, and I nearly quailed, but didn't quite.

"What is Uncle Frank doing there? Is he crossing the Great Australian Desert?"

He cleared his throat loudly. "For aught I know. He may do what he likes."

"Because Papa thought he was going to settle there, and if he met a lady whom he liked, he might divorce Mary, or she him, and he could have an heir for Blakemere."

Grandpapa looked down to the meadow, and at Richard's desultory play, then looked back at me, his eyes dim but angry.

"Oh, no," he said. "Frank will have no more heirs to Blakemere. Robert! *Robert*! Where is the man?"

And Robert came out and wheeled him into the house. I went back to Richard, but I looked across the river to the little wood in the distance. Oh, Frank was Down Under all right, I thought, only he wasn't ten thousand miles away. It was the first time I remember having a thought of such a grimly humorous turn. My life at Blakemere, my experience of the Fearing family, generated many such thoughts in the future.

I found out later that, some months before, my grandfather had changed his will again: minor bequests apart he left everything to my father and then, failing male heirs to him, to me. No mention was made of the estate's or the Bank's future after me. That was left entirely in my hands. I don't know if that was an expression of confidence in me, or one of total bemusement as to what was for the best. But certainly it bound me, tight.

My grandfather's decline was longer than he or anyone would have wanted. He died in March 1896, and my father was head of Fearing's Bank and master of Blakemere. And I was his heir.

CHAPTER TEN

THE NEW BROOM

My father decidedly took to running the Fearing empire.

He did not, in those early days, significantly change the routines followed year after year by my grandfather. He spent Monday to Thursday in London, staying at a suite in the Savoy, attending diligently to bank affairs by day, dining lavishly and attending light theatrical performances (that was the appeal of the Savoy) in the evenings. On Thursdays, after the bank closed, he came down to Blakemere and stayed till early Monday morning—enjoying shooting, golf, and the traditional hospitality for people who mattered that the Fearings had always gone in for. I remember from that time Mr. Asquith (as the coming man) and Joseph Chamberlain, as well as an awkward evening with Thomas Hardy and H. M. Stanley, who seemed to have little in common except a love of vast, unpopulated places. I began to attend, you notice, these dinners, though I resisted any attempts to make me Blakemere's hostess. I intended to go to University. I was becoming a serious, purposeful young lady.

My grandmother decided that she had done her duty by Blakemere and Fearing's Bank. It had always, I suspect, been duty, intermixed with little pleasure. She decided to spend her last years in charitable work in London, and in pleasure in the south of France and Italy.

My father asked Aunt Jane to be his hostess at Blakemere. It was an uninspired choice but a wise one. Aunt Jane was used to a place some way down the table, but she knew all the routines of the house and its hospitality: its aims and purposes were clear to her and unquestioned, and if she never sparkled she also never put a foot wrong. My father gave her a dramatically increased dress allowance, and if to modern eyes she would look comically frumpish—like, though one can't say so, Queen Mary today—in the 1890's she looked dignified and right.

Who persuaded my mother to leave Blakemere I do not know. Maybe Jane, maybe Grandmama, maybe even my father. Anyway, the embarrassment of her presence was removed: she was set up in an independent establishment in Torquay, and left with a simple "good-bye" to me. She occasionally indulged in whist with other elderly ladies, was now and then wheeled along the Front, but mostly, I believe, she cosseted her invalidism. She was looked after by a gentlewoman in reduced circumstances, who I hope was not unkind to her. On the other hand, I can think of no very good reason why she should have been especially kind.

So my father, Claudius Meyer Fearing, the third of his dynasty, rather flourished in his new state. At the Bank, or with other bankers, his opinion was respected—not perhaps as much as my grandfather's, but respected as that of one who knew what he was talking about. At Blakemere he was assured of automatic respect and obedience, but I soon became aware, through my network of relationships below stairs, that he received a good deal more than that. He was an example of the position making the man. He no longer had the air of being somehow superfluous.

I have just returned from visiting Edith—Miss Roxby that was, Mrs. Beale as she became. She is a sad case now, rambling without sense of purpose, now proposing to expound on the corn belt in North America, now conjugating irregular French verbs, sometimes sliding on to matters of a more embarrassing kind. This came on quite quickly after Robert died—they were for many years an odd but devoted couple. Seeing her in that nursing home, which tries to be cheery but has an inevitable underlying grimness, sent my mind back to the announcement of her proposed marriage. Now she is eighty-eight, then she was in her late thirties. It was by no means a conventional match—in fact, at the time it was potentially scandalous.

I did not fully understand this in 1896, soon after the death of my grandfather. When Edith told me privately, my comment was unintentionally tactless.

"I suppose you're married in all but name already," I said.

I was sixteen, but I think I had only very vague ideas about what "married in all but name" might imply. Miss Roxby bit her lip (I think with amusement rather than annoyance) and went on with her explanation. Not a great deal was needed. I knew, and the whole of Blakemere knew, that she and Robert saw a great deal of each other on their free days; and I knew, and below stairs at Blakemere knew, that even in the house they saw a great deal more of each other than a footman and a governess would normally do. It seemed to me perfectly natural that they should decide to get married.

It was some days before I realized that this was not the general opinion. I think I got the message from the pursed lips of Aunt Jane, reinforced by the raised eyebrows of Cousin Anselm, on a visit with his two sons while his wife was in labor. Both reactions told me there was something odd, off-key, *wrong* about the proposed marriage.

It was, of course, a matter of class. Miss Roxby was in an ambiguous position, somewhere between servant and family, but the official line was that she was a gentlewoman in reduced circumstances, and certainly *not* a servant. Robert had had the minimum education that the state provided, was the son of one of those men who had moved the earth to form the Blakemere estate, and thus was what we now confidently call working class.

"What will they find to talk about?" asked Aunt Jane.

Ignorant as I was, I knew enough to go away and have a good giggle.

It was some time before I, too, began to think there was something odd about the marriage, and that it was not a matter of class. Miss Roxby was to start a school in Wentwood, and, after prolonged and anguished suing on my part, it was agreed that I would attend it, both for ordinary classes, and to receive special tuition from a graduate (the word was spoken with bated breath) in mathematics, to fit me for the Cambridge Tripos. It was wonderfully exciting for me, the thought of mixing for the first time with real people (by which I meant not family and not hangers-on).

I realize now that my attendance was also symbolic: it showed potential parents that the project, and therefore the marriage, were approved of (after mature consideration) by the great, the rich, the powerful Fearing family.

"Isn't it grand?" I said to Edith, when I first saw Bankside School, two weeks before the September opening.

"It has to be quite big," said my former governess. "We aim to take quite a lot of boarders."

It was two substantial houses, with a newly constructed passage between them. The main bedrooms in the second house were large enough to form two substantial dormitories. The classrooms were on the ground floors of both houses, and the living quarters for Edith and Robert were in the upstairs part of the first house. The grounds were extensive, and a tennis court had been constructed. Everything was of the first quality, and it was really most attractive for a school, suggesting that Edith had been planning such an establishment, or perhaps just dreaming of it, for many years.

How could they afford this?

The question occurred to me after my first two weeks of school, when I had been well taught, well protected, and well fed at my midday meal. I was wandering around on my own—I enjoyed the unaccustomed experience of mixing with other girls, but I needed solitude now and then because I had so often been used to it. I was waiting for the carriage to come and fetch me back to Blakemere. It was not until the next year, my last, that I was allowed to catch the train. I was in the pleasant and well-cared-for grounds at the back of the two houses, gazing pensively up at the two stone structures, marveling at the extent of the enterprise.

Robert could have saved little from his wages—enough, perhaps, to give him some little preëminence in a rural environment, but not enough to contribute anything meaningful to a set-up such as Bankside School. Miss Roxby was well paid by governess standards, a hundred pounds a year, but such free time as she did not spend with her surviving sister she used to go up to London, to plays, concerts, and opera. I did not get the idea that she was a great saver, and even if she were—*this*?

I talked to Robert when I had got my ideas clearer in my head. Robert was Bankside School's man—functions vague but various. He could be general handyman when there was call for one, but at any time when parents might call he was well dressed, imposing, and a deferential but confidence-building front. He was the girls' and teachers' escort when outside the school. He could also impose order. Many girls fell in love with him, but all hopelessly. Few troublemakers ever got the better of him.

"Is the school going well, Robert?" I asked him, as he stood surveying the girls in the grounds during a recreation period.

"Quite nicely, thank you, Miss Sarah," he replied complacently. "Two new girls starting next week. Parents not happy with the school they're attending at the moment. They'd heard good things about Bankside."

"That must be very gratifying."

"Oh, it is, Miss Sarah. Mrs. Beale is very happy about the way things are going."

"How *lucky* you were," I said, gushing a little, "to be able to set up a wonderful place like this when you got married."

"Ah, well, you see, Miss Sarah, Edith and I were a lot later than most in getting wed."

I said nothing, and he seemed to find the pause awkward. "And I don't mind saying that your family were very helpful, in view of our long service at Blakemere."

"That was very generous of them."

"A loan, o' course, but on good terms, and very welcome and timely."

His manner had less than its usual confidence. I meditated on this, and on his words, during the carriage ride home that day. It seemed to me that Robert would have let me think that, due to their unusually mature years at marriage, he and Edith had acquired the property and equipped it as a school out of their savings if I had not left that pause. It had then occurred to him that he was talking to a young lady who intended to go to Cambridge to study mathematics, and possibly a future head of Fearing's Bank to boot. He then amended his account to praise my family's generosity and then—sensing a degree of skepticism—had amended this once again to describe it as a loan. Interesting.

I considered this whole account, wondering whether my family was really generous to its retainers. Only so-so, I thought, though they were paid well, a fact that was resented by other employers of domestic labor in the vicinity. I wondered, too, whether Miss Roxby's ten-year service could really be described as "long," and whether Robert's service, starting low-down and ending as a mere under-footman, was so very special.

But most of all I meditated my waking nightmare of the time of Uncle Frank's disappearance, and that view from above of a shape that I thought was Robert's, holding the lantern beside the stretcher that bore a long shape covered by a dark rug.

I found I could not discuss this with Edith: we shared our thoughts on matters of moment, we were unrestrained in each other's company, we liked each other—yet we were not intimate. And even if we were, could I have approached a subject that might have amounted to an accusation of blackmail: that they had used Robert's involvement in the disposal of Uncle Frank's body to screw money out of my family? It was out of the question.

I meditated, as I say, long and hard. I decided that the only person to whom I might broach such a topic—and then only cautiously—was Beatrice. I waited two days or so, trying to get the situation right in my mind, then went to see her and Richard on a fine Saturday in early October. We had decided to leave Richard with Bea another year, then bring him back to Blakemere. Watching him playing with the South children (another was on the way, as usual) made me sure we had come to the right decision. However, Beatrice sounded a note of caution.

"It may not be for the best for him to stay here much longer," she said.

I looked at her in surprise: she did not often change her mind.

"Tom is getting cussed."

"Cussed?"

"Bad tempered. Doesn't like children around his feet the whole time."

"Well, he's got a funny way of showing it, Bea." I said, nodding toward her belly. We both giggled. "Anyway, Blakemere is full of cussed people."

"But he can be kept away from them. Never need see them. Here he gets upset by the bad atmosphere." My heart lifted with love as I looked toward his puffy, slow-eyed face, and saw the consideration of Bea's eldest as he adapted his play to suit the boy. "Mind you, he soon forgets it when Tom's out of the way," Bea went on. "And anyway, Blakemere's a much happier place now, isn't it?"

"I suppose so," I considered, almost surprised. "Yes, something has made a difference, and I suppose it must be Papa, and Mother leaving, and all the changes. But I did want him to come back during the summer holidays, when I have all my time to give him."

"But you'll have another year's school after that, and then Cambridge. You'll need someone there to look after him and love him."

"Of course."

"Well, think on't. Have you considered that Bertha?"

We chewed over this for some time. Typically for Bea it was an instinctive but a brilliant suggestion, as time proved. Bertha looked after Richard literally as if he was her own. We had ranged in our conversation over that and related matters when finally I said, "You should see Edith's new school, Bea. She and Robert have really done themselves proud. Two large houses with lots of grounds, and 'beautifully appointed,' as the advertisements say."

Bea nodded, unsuspecting.

"That's nice. I thought you might find a school pokey, after what you've been used to."

"Beautiful pokiness!" I laughed. I added prophetically: "If I ever own Blakemere, I'm going to live in the coach house or the gatehouse. Then I'll let that awful barn of a place to . . . to . . ." But my imagination failed me.

"The King of Siam and all his wives," suggested Bea.

We both laughed.

"It *is* difficult to think who'd want it," I conceded. "But Bea, how would Edith and Robert have found the money to start a splendid spic-and-span new school like Bankside?"

Her manner seemed to take on a degree of caginess.

"How would I know? Maybe she came into some money."

"She doesn't have rich relatives. Anyway, she would have told me. We talk about things like that. . . . Robert says the money came from my family."

"There you are, then."

"That sort of generosity doesn't sound like them."

"The Fearings are not 'them,' they're 'us' to you, Miss Sarah. And you won't hear many below stairs complaining about them."

"I know that. But if they—we—handed out a big sum like that must have been to anyone we'd employed, it would generally be a quid pro quo."

"Don't be throwing those foreign tongues at me, Miss Sarah."

It was a common complaint with Bea, but it sounded like a dodging tactic.

"I mean, we don't generally give anything for nothing."

"Not many people do."

"Maybe not. And I suppose we wouldn't be bankers if we did . . . What do they say in the servants' hall happened on the night Uncle Frank went away?"

"What do you bring that up for?"

"I want to know. You know how I loved Uncle Frank."

She looked down at her lap, or her rounded belly.

"They say there was some kind of . . . of violence, like . . . and Mr. Frank had to leave double quick."

"I see. What kind of violence?"

"Nobody knows. But the family took it so serious they wouldn't have nothing more to do with him, not ever. Like maybe he hit his wife."

"Hmmm," I said skeptically. "I admire them for taking it so

seriously if it was that. I've never heard of any trouble the from Coverdales about it."

"Happen it was all hushed up. But I'll tell you what else they say."

"What?"

"They say it's something better not talked about, better not looked into. There's something of that sort in all families, as you'd know if you were a bit older and a bit more knowledgeable in the ways of the world. Let sleeping dogs lie—homely advice, but good."

I think in the long run her homely advice influenced me. I was beginning not to forget Uncle Frank, but to get over his loss. I was starting to think about going up to Cambridge, and about what I was to do after that. And I suppose this accounts for the fact that my pursuit of the truth of Uncle Frank's death was distinctly desultory and unsuccessful, even when I was head of the Fearings and mistress of Blakemere. I had my own life to lead, and it was a life that involved many hard decisions.

Alas, I missed entirely Bea's oblique allusion to herself in what she said, and to her own marriage. Not that I could have done anything about that when Bea put up with it so uncomplainingly for the sake of the children. I made one more attempt at that time—my seventeenth year—to find out the truth about That Night. It was in the entrance hall at Bankside School, and I had just arrived from Blakemere. By now Robert and I were firm friends, and I often gave him little snippets of news from his old home, about the people there.

"Papa was very thoughtful at breakfast today," I said.

"Oh, dear, Miss Sarah. Not trouble at the Bank, I hope."

"No, it couldn't be. Papa was there yesterday. He got a letter with a foreign stamp on it. I think it must have been from Uncle Frank."

Robert jumped a fraction, then with an effort resumed his calm passivity.

"I didn't know your uncle still kept in touch with his family."

"Nor did I. I didn't like to ask Papa about it. Is it true Uncle Frank went to Australia, Robert?"

"Of course it is, Miss Sarah. He was unhappy in his marriage and he went to Australia. You were told about that, I'm sure. Why do you ask me? I was just a servant at Blakemere."

"Servants often know more than family—especially young people like me."

"Well, I only know what I was told. Your uncle is in Australia. It's a long, long way away, Miss Sarah. I shouldn't bank on him ever coming back if I were you."

That was all I got out of him. Robert was always splendidly impassive. If those last words were a coded message, it was one he could easily deny: I was jumping to conclusions like any silly girl was apt to. It was very seldom, in all the years I knew him, those years of my friendship with Edith and him, that I got anything of substance out of him.

I thought about these things on the way home from visiting poor Edith. How lucky Robert was, to have died first, though the younger. And how Edith would have hated being in her present condition, if she could be conscious of it. Would we in this country, I wondered, ever legalize euthanasia?

At the gatehouse there were boxes from London. I was in for a hard, boring evening. There was also a letter from cousin Digby Fearing at the Bank: long and dry about banking matters, with some personal details at the end. He has a dull, loving wife and two children, of whom the boy is promising to be a high-flyer in the Conservative Party ("I shouldn't say this to you, but . . ."). To blow the cobwebs away before putting a meal together and then getting down to work I decided to take the dogs for their walk—indeed, my relationship with them is such that I had no choice: humans I can command, and have done so from a quite early age; dogs I obey.

I had nearly used up my petrol ration, so we went the familiar way up to the house. That monstrous, sprawling bulk with all its innumerable windows securely boarded up is an almost frightening sight—if one notices. I hardly do. Blakemere, in one state of another, has always been *there* in my life. To the dogs it just seems something to go *around*—a monstrous obstacle between smells and more smells. Lizzie, the old dog, has forgotten she ever lived there, and is infinitely happier in the smaller, cozier, warmer gatehouse. Ernie, the younger but fatter dog, has never been inside.

Meditating on this blind hulk in the midst of a vibrant landscape rich in wildlife, thrilling for the dogs, I realize that Blakemere is now dead. By the locals it is not forgotten, but it is discounted: it is no longer of any moment. It is as dead as Uncle Frank, who someone, somehow, killed in the red sitting room and buried in the little wood which I could see in the distance, basking in the late sunlight over on the horizon.

CHAPTER ELEVEN

FALSE START

To go up to Cambridge in 1898 was to enter an institution where women were accepted but unwanted. They themselves were so aware of this, so desperate to be wanted and valued, that the college principals and academics fenced girls in with so many rules and prohibitions that they were hard put to find a way off the rails even when they had a mind to it.

Nevertheless, for me it was liberation.

It was no more family, no more Blakemere. But it was more positive than that as well: it was friends who were my intellectual equals, it was teachers who were penetrating thinkers (*some*—and the ones who were not, I avoided), it was sitting in libraries and it was going shopping, it was attending exciting new plays at theaters, it was singing in the college choir, it was circumventing regulations and, just occasionally, talking to a man about men's matters without his displaying condescension or surprise.

When the end of my first term approached I sent a note to Mrs. Merton, the Blakemere housekeeper, telling her when I would be arriving back. When the end of my second term came near, as an experiment, I wrote a note to my father, ending it "Your loving daughter Sarah." Somewhat to my surprise I received a reply. It was a hand-tinted postcard of one of the stars of the Doyly Carte Opera, typewritten on the back, doubtless by one of the Bank's secretaries—a new breed of employee, representing a new if subservient role for women. The note read:

> Will be delighted to see you again. Place not the same without you. Would invite eminent mathematicians for weekend if knew any. You will have to make do with bankers and politicians.
>
> Your loving father
> Claud Fearing

The postcard, which my father seemed to have written as if he was composing a telegram, was enclosed in a conventional bank envelope. As the picture represented the star dancing a cachucha, fandango, or bolero with lots of frilly skirts it would otherwise have caused scandal at Newnham. My papa obviously understood these things better than I would have given him credit for. I replied:

> Bankers and politicians quite acceptable. Used to them.
>
> All my love,
> Sarah

Sadly I could find no postcard even mildly risqué in Cambridge. This could well be because I did not know where to look. I sent one of young men in boaters punting on the Backs.

My relationship with my father, you will have realized, was changing. Now I was on the verge of being "grown up" he began to value my company, talked to me a lot, introduced me with pride to Blakemere's guests. It was not till my Cambridge years were over, however, that he would use phrases of introduction such as "The future head of the family," or "the future mistress of Blakemere," or even "the future head of Fearing's Bank." That, at the turn of the century, was an idea that few could take in—few men, that is, and not a great many more women. We forget, these days, how many prominent women there were foolish enough even to oppose female suffrage.

Actually they are still around. They are the sort of women who in the war opposed the Land Army, and found its women workers unwomanly and reprehensible.

Aunt Jane remained hostess at Blakemere, and I only stepped in during her occasional illness. It was not a role I coveted, though I relished many of my encounters with politicians: it was the age of Balfour, but also of Lloyd George—he being a coming man, and therefore courted by Fearing's Bank in spite of his lowly origins and dubious moral character.

But my vacations at Blakemere meant, above all, Richard. He was at home permanently now, and in the charge of Bertha, the slow but loving housemaid, newly promoted and properly paid, and taking wonderful and constant care of him. Richard was growing up: physically the process was unmistakable, mentally it was less so. He had long periods of contented lethargy, broken by spells of joy, activity, simple pleasure in people and things around him. He loved me unreservedly (was he the first human being to do so?), and in return I made him one of the centers of my universe. He was a person for whom one could only make the simplest of plans, and that was indeed a happiness and a relief. There had always been too much plotting and planning, too much trying to nudge Providence, at Blakemere. We were never content to lie back in the water and let the wave take us. Even my father was not immune to this family trait.

"Who do you anticipate inheriting Blakemere if you have no family?" he asked me one day, when I was indulging in a fashionable feminist diatribe against men.

I shrugged. "Probably one of Cousin Anselm's sons," I said. "I can't see one of Clare's taking over, can you?"

Aunt Clare's (wholly delightful) collection of sons were beginning rackety careers that included music-hall performing, ballooning, commercial traveling, on-course bookmaking, and dabbling in dubious transactions that led to prudent and hurried emigration. Aunt Clare and Uncle Alfred were burned to death two years later in a fire at their home-cum-studio, in which an awful lot of bad paintings were also destroyed. They were buried in Chelsea, rather than in the newish Fearing family vault in Wentwood Church.

"Yes," my father nodded, "it does look as if it will all have to come to one of them. And Digby seems a lot more reliable than his father. But I hope you'll get married."

"I haven't worked out my attitude to men yet," I said, as if the world was waiting. "If only I could find myself a young man like Uncle Frank."

"I blame myself about Frank," said my father, after a pause.

That was all he said, and something in the set of his shoulders told me to pursue the subject no further that day. I did approach the subject of Frank now and then with my father, but this was the closest I ever got to a statement of his share in the responsibility. I got no details ever of the last night Frank spent at Blakemere, or anything beyond the family line about where he was. My father registered my curiosity, but never satisfied it. One day over breakfast—a meal we generally shared alone—he read a letter, then pocketed it, saying, "That was from your aunt Mary. Funny woman. She seems to repel sympathy."

I agreed with *that* wholeheartedly.

"What is she doing?"

"Looking after an aged relative in Dumfries. Doesn't need to—gets a splendid annual income from us. Wants to be a martyr, I suppose. Bit of a hypochondriac, too."

"Like Mama."

"Yes, like your mother. Though that went well beyond hypochondria."

If I had not then worked out my attitude to men, I soon began to do so. One of the pleasures of being at Cambridge was that occasionally, usually at the beginning or the end of term, I could spend a weekend with my grandmother in London, doing the things she loved and wanted me to love too: going to plays, galleries, and museums, holding or going to intimate dinners (so different from Blakemere's dinners) where a few intelligent people discussed topics of current interest. My grandmother, I sensed, had bloomed, and was enjoying life more than ever before. When I was in my last year at Cambridge she proposed that I should spend a week or ten days with her at Easter in the south of France: a party was going from Bankside

School, she said, so Edith Beale could be my chaperone on the journey. The girls and their headmistress would be staying at a small pensionnat in Nice, but I would of course stay with her. I was overjoyed, and I think felt just a little flattered.

I joined the party at Waterloo. The girls were loomed over and shepherded by Robert, now becoming portly, but immensely intimidating should intrusion or impertinence threaten the little party. Edith, too, was putting on weight, but she was the respectable and efficient school principal to the life. How long ago it seemed, when I had listened to Robert's footsteps in the corridor outside our bedrooms, and how the twelve young ladies in the party would have enjoyed hearing about it!

"Sarah!" said Edith, kissing me. "It's wonderful to see you again—and looking so well."

I shook hands with Robert and was introduced to all of the girls. I was a little ashamed to admit that this was just as big an adventure for me as it was for them, so I assumed a world-wise pose, and it was only as we were going through Customs at Dover that I wondered whether the pose would survive my first experience of sea travel.

By a miracle it did. I experienced no discomfort at all. It has always been a great joy to me—even, foolishly, a pride—that I can keep my stomach when all around are losing theirs. It was when most of the girls were below deck, suffering grievously, or foolishly pretending to, that on the breezy deck in weak sunshine a young man approached me.

"It is a beautiful day, is it not?"

A young Frenchman! Heaven! The traditional trap for the virginal English girl. I saw Robert moving away from his wife, who was looking queasy, and coming to stand close by.

"Quite perfect for a sea trip."

"Mademoiselle does not suffer from sea-illness?"

"Sea-*sickness*," I said, before I could stop myself. I had foreign friends at Cambridge who always wanted their English corrected. The man just nodded. "No, I don't. It's a great boon to have that sort of constitution."

"You are going to Paris?"

"To the south—Nice. And you?"

This last question, I'll have you know, was very forward, even brash, for a young lady at the turn of the century: one did not question a young man about himself.

"To Marseilles. And yours—it is a pleasure trip?"

"Purely pleasure. And yours?"

"One does not go to Marseilles for pleasure."

I smiled, he murmured, "Charles de Maurras, at your service, mademoiselle," and removed himself to another part of the deck. I think, in retrospect, I should have asked myself why he had not asked my name. In retrospect, I think it was because he already knew it.

He was there again when we got to the Gare St. Lazare, and we talked while Robert was busy with porters and luggage, and while Edith, though nearby, was occupied with shepherding her flock and answering their questions. Her flock's eyes were mostly on me, instinct with curiosity, and I suspect that many of their questions to her and affectations of nervousness were designed to keep their headmistress's attention elsewhere than on us. Girls had to stick together in those days.

He told me he was in the cotton trade, was returning from Bolton and Burnley, where he had business, and now had to report back to his Marseilles firm before he could hope for a few days' holiday. He asked my name, perhaps realizing his earlier mistake, asked why I was traveling with a school party when I was clearly beyond school age, expressed wonderment that I was studying at the world-renowned University of Kembritch. When Robert had sorted out the matter of the luggage he engaged the young man in conversation for a minute or two, but soon M. de Maurras bowed and left to catch a different train.

He appeared in Nice on our second day there.

I realize I am relating an incident wholly predictable, one irrelevant to the matter in hand, except in so far as I figure in it. I am telling it to you simply because it was a determining incident in my life. There were also matters of some interest as side issues, in particular the attitude and behavior of Edith and Robert.

It had been tacitly assumed that I would, when not with my grandmama, go around with the school party and receive the extremely efficient chaperonage that they were given. With the reappearance of Charles de Maurras (the "de" was self-assumed, I feel quite sure) the situation tacitly changed. He came up to us on a visit to an art gallery, and engaged not just me but Edith and Robert in conversation. By the time the gallery visit ended we had an assignation for the next day. I told Edith I was engaged with Grandmama, and she made no attempt to verify the assertion. From then on she and Robert turned a blind eye to what was going on, though they certainly saw us around.

What was their motive in this? It is possible that Charles slipped them some money, but I doubt it: they had no need of it, and if it were found out, it would ruin their relationship with the family and probably destroy their school. I think they decided I was twenty-one, and it was time I was initiated into a side of life from which they themselves derived unashamed pleasure. I think they thought it was time I began the process of deciding what place what we today simply call sex was to have in my life. If so, the decision came quicker than they could have anticipated.

It was after our second session in a hotel bedroom—seedier than I was used to, but not the less exciting for that, at least first time round—when, after that all-purpose word sex, and after thanks and endearments, Charles began talking about banks and money with considerably more interest and enthusiasm than he ever could muster about me, that I made up my mind.

"I must go," I said, and got up and began dressing.

"Tomorrow, *ma chère*? Two o'clock?"

I nodded. I think by the time I let myself out of the shabby room he had registered my lack of enthusiasm, so it may have been small surprise to him when I did not appear in our usual meeting place at two o'clock. I never saw him again. He later went into politics, and had a minor ministry in the Pétain government. We didn't bother to shoot him, so he is probably even now preparing the way for a return to political life. How odd if we should meet officially!

My grandmother, for the rest of my stay, had the pleasure of a great deal of my company, probably rather more than she wished for. Sometimes, though, usually in the early evenings, I would take myself off and walk on the promenade or on the beach. I thought about men, and though I did not decide to forswear them entirely, I did decide they were to have no more than a marginal place in my life. Sex was pleasant enough—no more. Not something to give up my controlling interest in myself for.

Which left me with—what?

One possible answer was the Bank and the house. It wasn't what I wanted, but it was what I had got, or would get in the future, if I accepted it. It may seem like an odd choice, but remember there were many women who would count me lucky beyond belief to have such wealth, and the possibility of such a fascinating occupation. And by heading Fearing's Bank, even if only by inheritance, I could blaze a trail for other women. I still thought, you notice, in the metaphors of explorers and empire builders.

"I don't think men are going to be very important in my life," I said to my grandmother, as we sat over coffee at the end of a fine dinner, toward the end of my stay.

"*Men?*" she said disapprovingly. "I presume you mean the man you marry, or don't marry."

"I suppose I do."

"And what will you do if you don't marry?"

"Run the Bank and be mistress of Blakemere, as Grandpapa wanted in his will."

"If you run the Bank, men will certainly be *very* important in your life," my grandmother pointed out, with reason.

"I mean in my personal life," I explained. "Marriage. I think a man would only get in the way. I don't think I'd want to give too much time to one."

"In that case, you certainly should not marry. A man always takes a lot of a woman's time, though he doesn't always give her a great deal of his own."

"Apart from you and Grandpapa, I'm not sure our family's cut out for marriage. Look at Papa and Mama, look at Uncle Frank. I think Aunt Jane and Aunt Sarah were wise."

Grandmama raised her eyebrows.

"Your aunt Sarah never had an offer, and your aunt Jane had romantic notions that prevented her accepting the one offer she did have. If your grandfather's and my marriage was . . ." She paused, and I knew at once what word she was rejecting, "successful, it was because I knew my place—an old-fashioned idea these days, but it worked. In public I supported him absolutely, in private I might influence him, but it was best to be indirect, to lead without seeming to, to flatter him."

"What sort of ways did you influence him in?"

She thought.

"My people, the Jewish background I came from, has always been interested in money, but also in using it well, for the community, for people in need. My successes were modest, but I think I helped a little in that direction, because your grandfather was not naturally charitable."

I thought a lot about that later on.

"And what went wrong, do you think, with Papa's marriage, and Uncle's?"

She shrugged.

"Who can tell the truth about another person's marriage? Your mother was—is—a poor creature. I don't need to mince my words with you. She had her moment of glory, at the marriage, and later when she was pregnant. But underneath she was trivial and selfish. Hers is a life hardly worth living."

"And Uncle Frank?"

Incipient tension now showed itself in her body.

"What about him? You know the marriage was a disaster."

"Do you regret forcing him into it?"

"Forcing? He was a grown man. He made the decision . . . But I do regret that we offered him inducements. He was quite irresponsible with money, and money should have been cut off. You can't make people responsible about money by offering them more."

"The conditions were hard."

"What do you know about it, young lady? He could have married any young woman he chose—anyone acceptable. Choosing Mary Coverdale was choosing to sail toward disaster."

"Do you think he has learned his lesson? Is he making a new life for himself in Australia?"

"I have no idea. He does not communicate with us, and we don't communicate with him. And that is all I am going to say on the subject, my girl."

She was perhaps wise to close the topic, because I was going to ask whether a total break with the most attractive of her children was not a disproportionate punishment both for herself and him for the failure of his marriage. But I knew, anyway, that the total break was due to death, and I certainly did not think it was of her doing.

I meditated on these things as I drove to Wentwood to dispatch my boxes back to London. There is a tiny bit more traffic on the roads now, with the coming of summer and people finding ways of fiddling the petrol rationing. I nearly had a minor collision at a country cross roads, and I stopped dreaming of the past and concentrated on what I was doing. On the way back I exercised Lizzie and Ernie on Wybush Common. The woman—the shrew—I'd had the altercation with was in her garden, but she merely turned away when Lizzie dashed through it. *She knows who I am*, I thought, *and that's why she's holding her tongue*. But was it the mistress of Blakemere or the public figure who intimidated her? I decided it was probably the latter.

Back in the gatehouse I parked the car and fixed the waterproof cover over it. It's just too far from the stables to make it worthwhile parking it there. I was straightening up when I saw that there was a figure walking down the long path from Blakemere. That was unusual. The grounds are in effect open (all the cast-iron gates and railings went to make munitions during the war), but few take advantage of the fact. Someone interested in Victorian architecture? I wondered. There are one or two signs that the art and buildings of the nineteenth century are poised to make a modest comeback. This was a young person, though, with a rucksack on his or her back. . . . His. A young man, tanned, a good walker. As he approached I thought how rude I was to stare: I didn't mind if he made free of the Blakemere grounds. I turned toward the front door of the gatehouse, but I was hailed.

"I say, excuse me. Are you Sarah Fearing?"

I turned back.

"Yes."

"I've come to say hello. I'm a sort of distant cousin of yours."

It was as if a large cold hand suddenly gripped and held my spine. His accent was broad Australian.

CHAPTER TWELVE

VISITOR

That feeling of a cold hand with a grip that held my whole body was still with me as I said, my voice not entirely steady:

"Well, you'd better come in . . . er . . . ?"

"Edmund. Everyone calls me Ed."

"Australians don't like two-syllable names, do they?" I realized I'd put on my "making conversation" voice as I led the way into the pokey but welcoming little gatehouse. "A cup of tea? Some orange squash? Lemonade?"

"Tea would be fine. This doesn't really count as a fine day for an Australian."

Preparing tea gave me a chance to regain my cool. In the little kitchen, clattering cups and jugs and sugar bowls, I shook off the grip of the chilly hand. Clare's son had gone to Australia, hadn't he? Now which one was it? The second one, I thought. What on earth was his name? Her children had become a sort of blur in my mind over the years—they were people of whom one heard vague rumors from time to time, either funny or disquieting ones. Round about 1903, I thought, this one had emigrated. This young man could be his son—or even his grandson. He had not been married at the time he left England, after the affair of the bogus share certificates. Ed could well take after him. He was not good-looking, at least not yet, but his smile suggested he would one day be able to charm the birds from the trees.

"I just realized," said the boy's voice from the kitchen door, "I suppose tea is rationed, isn't it? Is there something I could have that isn't?"

"Tea is fine," I assured him.

"I suppose you can fiddle a bit in your position."

"In my position I can't fiddle at all. The newspapers would be down on me like a ton of bricks."

"I suppose so," the boy conceded. "It would be the same in Australia. Tall poppies and all that."

"Tall poppies?"

"People in authority getting above themselves."

"Quite right, too. That's a very healthy attitude. We are the sort of people who should be watched. I rather like the idea of being a tall poppy. Milk? Sugar? Please don't say no to spare my rations."

"Yes, then, to both." He grinned. His voice, twang and all, was rather attractive, his grin even more so. "Can I carry the tray through?"

When we had gone through to the little sitting room, he put the tray carefully on a small side table over by the window, then stood up to his beanpole height and looked around. "Must be a change after the place up there," he said.

"It is."

"A comedown."

I shook my head vigorously. "Not at all. Just somewhere where it's much pleasanter and more comfortable to live. The war gave me the opportunity to do what I'd always wanted: shut up that great barn."

"What I couldn't work out," he said seriously, "walking round it, is: what was it filled up *with*? What were all the rooms *for?*"

"It never was filled up. Oh, almost, I suppose, if there was a *very* large houseparty, or if the Prime Minister and his entourage stayed there at election time. But normally only a fraction of the place was used. Furnished, but not used."

"I couldn't see the rooms, of course. Are they the normal size?"

"No. Inflated. Most of them were the normal size times three or four."

"Upward as well?"

"Upward as well—at least on the ground floor."

"Not real cozy."

"Not cozy at all. Cold, drafty, and somehow . . . dwarfing. You felt small there. Irrelevant. Good for the soul maybe. But I hated it."

"Why good for the soul?"

"Because it was built to glorify the Fearings, and all we did in it was feel small."

"But not when you were entertaining those grand houseparties, I shouldn't think."

"I never did. Luckily by the time I took over they were a thing of the past."

Even my father had not been the sort of man to relish playing Master of Blakemere at large, lavish houseparties. We had a medium-sized one once a year in the years before what I think of as the Great War. This was the only piece of entertaining Aunt Jane had to do where she felt slightly out of her depth, or at least out of her element. During those weekends, and reluctantly, I took on some of the hostess's duties.

Richard loved these parties, and I always insisted he be introduced to people, allowed to play a part in the games and other activities when he could. Most of the guests were polite and friendly toward him. Those who were not, and especially those who had to hide a revulsion, I noted down, and they were not asked to Blakemere again.

I was by now working at the Bank. I had had a few months at home after University, then embarked on a continental tour, with a chaperone. I should have chosen someone like Edith, someone with backbone, but I didn't. Two months in, at Vienna, I found my companion intolerably insipid, the foreign cities tedious in bulk, travel itself distasteful. I cancelled the rest of the tour, returned to Blakemere and told my father he had to find something for me to do at Fearing's Bank.

So when we had these (by our standards) modest houseparties they were busy weekends in the midst of a busy but challenging working life in London. One didn't always know precisely who would be there. This was particularly so when, as often happened as I took over more of the work from my father, I left the business of receiving the guests to Aunt Jane and only came down to Blakemere on the Saturday morning.

I remember one such party, in the heyday of Asquith, before the suffragette agitation became really violent, when I came down late in this way, greeted Richard, who was waiting for me on the stairs as I used to wait for Uncle Frank, and then, when we had hugged and laughed ourselves into a state of weariness, went out with him and Bertha on to the lawns and watched some of the guests playing croquet, with a little knot of spectators standing around them.

"Everything going well?" I asked Bertha.

"Oh, yes, miss. Everyone very happy as usual. Many of the gentlemen are out shooting."

"Of course." I suddenly stiffened. "Who's that?"

My eye had been caught by a shape in one of the little knots of spectators—the set of a woman's shoulders, a glimpse of her profile. Mr. McKay, still butler, though becoming a touch arthritic, had come up behind us.

"That's Mrs. Louisa Brackenbury. Louisa Coverdale as was, Miss Sarah," he said quietly.

"For a moment I thought—"

"The resemblance to her sister is striking."

"I would not be happy if her sister Mary was invited here."

He shot me a kind of look that people describe as "old-fashioned."

"I'm sure your father and your aunt Jane would understand your feelings on the point, Miss Sarah."

"And of course she wouldn't want to come," I said, feeling I'd been foolish.

I did not manage to speak to the former Louisa Coverdale in the course of the weekend. Or rather, I did not try very hard. The Coverdales were rarely at Tillyards in those days, and the place was already beginning to have a decrepit, unloved appearance. Peter was in the Army, the elder sister was with her husband on the Diplomatic

Corps round of foreign cities, Louisa was married, and the parents seemed to prefer living in London on the fashionable fringes of Society. When I went to Tillyards, I rarely went beyond the coachman's cottage, where Bea and her growing family were still a light in my life, and in Richard's. I had to ignore, because she insisted that I did, the occasional bruise or cut on her face. She never, I should add, expressed regret at her marriage. That would have meant regret for having her children, the rich delight of her life. They were part of a contract she had entered into with her eyes open. The bruises, nevertheless, made me rage inwardly.

The sight of such evidences of mistreatment meant that I never recanted on my decision not to marry, never thought wistfully about what it would be like to have children. In any case I had a child: I had Richard.

The boy Ed was tired that night, and after eliciting from me the assurance that putting him up for a night or two would be no trouble, and after conspicuously holding himself back from eating too much for dinner (he obviously felt that the English were living on iron rations, like an Antarctic expedition), he took himself amiably off to bed, expressing enormous gratitude for it—"first for three months, because I don't call a ship's bunk a bed"—and leaving his knapsack and most of its contents in an untidy heap in the corner of the gatehouse's little living room.

I hope I have not given the impression of being a sly, devious, underhand sort of person—at least not more so than a lonely, underoccupied childhood tended to make me. Nevertheless, I have to admit that the first thing I did when I was satisfied he had finished in the bathroom and settled in bed (splendid sound of ancient bedsprings creaking—the bed was from the servants' quarters at Blakemere, the ones from the house proper being too large for the gatehouse bedrooms) was to go over to the pile of dirty clothes, paperback books, guides, and heavy boots which formed the pile in the corner and rummage in it for the boy's passport and travel documents. Remember he had arrived out of nowhere, I hadn't the slightest idea who he was, and he had marked me down as a person of "position"—

though owning the empty hulk that is Blakemere makes me that, I suppose.

His name was Edmund Fearing Clements, and he had been born in Bathurst, New South Wales, in 1925. In an emergency the authorities were requested to contact Paul Edmund Clements of 25 Jacaranda Avenue, Bathurst. The photograph and description of him told me nothing I did not already know. His ticket told me that he had sailed from Sydney on the Stratheden on July 2.

When he came down the next morning, his sleep seemed to have released splendid resources of energy. He glowed.

"Is that for me?" he asked, seeing me at the stove, and smelling traditional smells. "Jeez, I'd rather you didn't. I feel indebted. I can fill up on toast."

"Nonsense, toast doesn't make a breakfast," I said. "And there'll be plenty of that, too. This is scrambled egg. It won't be the best you've ever tasted, because I only learned to cook when the war started and I moved here."

"Won't it use up your egg ration?"

"Hens. We've always had them at Blakemere. Now we just have a few, over by the stables. A nice woman from the village cycles up every day to feed them and collect the eggs. Here we are."

I spooned the eggs on to the toast, handed him his plate, and set some slices of bread in the toaster. Then I sat down at table with the strong coffee I preferred to start the day, and looked at the endearing young man.

"Good sleep?"

A broad smile illumined his face, like a lopsided crescent moon, and his fair hair flopped down over his forehead as he nodded enthusiastically.

"Wonderful! Don't remember a thing about it."

"Where have you been staying before?"

"Youth hostels, camping sites, places that did really cheap bed and breakfast. I only docked eight days ago."

"You didn't lost much time in coming over when the war ended."

"Why would I? I decided to take a year off before going to Uni. Where else would I go? I'm going to take in Europe as well."

"Currency may be a difficulty. And some parts where there's been heavy bombing are best avoided." I watched him spreading marmalade over two slices of toast and launch into the first of them. His activity didn't stop him taking in everything I said. "Did you do any wartime service?" I asked. He shook his head.

"No, only civilian backup. Unfit."

"You don't look in the least unfit to me."

"Asthma. Anyone can have it—athletes, and that. The physical standard's very high in the Australian army."

"I'm sure it is. What does today hold?"

"London."

"Not much you can do in a day."

" 'Course not. I'm prospecting—finding the sorts of places I can stay—youth hostels and that. Can't bludge on you for long. When I leave here I'll use a week or so to really do London over."

"That sounds wise."

"I'll try and get some good advice. The Aussies are starting to come back here this summer—not that many, because the papers back home go on about it still being pretty grim in the Old Country. But they say if I head for the Aldwych I'll find plenty of people my age in the hotels around there."

"Pubs, you mean?"

"Yeah, pubs. They'll all have tips. We're good at taking care of ourselves. I thought I'd head for the station at that little place near here."

"Melbury. Not all the trains stop there. There's one in half an hour, otherwise you'll have to get one of the little local trains to Wentwood and take a London train from there."

He looked at his watch and got up.

"Half an hour. I can just make it if I run."

"No—have another piece of toast and another cup of tea. Then I'll drive you there."

He accepted, saying, "Just this once," and stressed in the car that I wasn't to make a meal for him that night. When I got back to the gatehouse I took his knapsack and all his stuff up to his bedroom, and systematically went through it. I wondered why I did it, and decided it was the war that had made us all suspicious. Children all had a field day in those years spotting "spies" (usually picking on anyone who was in any way odd or outside the common herd), but in a milder way adults were the same. I was being visited by someone who said he was related to me, but who was news to me. He had not even volunteered so much as a surname when he claimed kinship. I wanted—and I suppose here I was reverting to a sort of Fearing tribalism—to know what he was to me.

But I found nothing that was in the least revealing as far as personal papers were concerned—no letters from his family, no half-written letters to them, no address book. I would have to ask him.

Ed got back about ten o'clock that night, and we sat up for an hour or so, drinking a milky nightcap and swapping events of the day.

"Met an old mate of mine, in a . . . a *pub* in the Strand," Ed said. "Used to live in Bathurst, just dropped out of Uni at Sydney to come over and see the Old Country. He and a few cobbers are going to buy an old car if that's possible—he says we'll have to pay over the odds—and take off for Europe in it. I think I'll be in on that. Too good an opportunity to miss."

"Much too good," I agreed. "But as I said, there'll be currency problems."

"Too right. Nothing but regulations. Suppose it's normal, all things considered. But we'll take tents—that way, the only expenses will be fuel and food."

"How long are you planning to stay over here?"

The boy frowned. "As long as I can, within reason. That will mean getting a job. What prospect of that, would you say?"

"Not too bad. There's none of the unemployment there was after the Great War, so you wouldn't be taking a job an ex-serviceman might have had."

"I hadn't thought of that," Ed admitted. "I suppose people would resent me if I did that."

"They would, but with full employment there's no problem. What sort of job were you thinking about?"

"Anything—laborer, farmworker, barman, commercial traveler. I can turn my hand to most things."

"It sounds as if you won't have much difficulty in getting fixed up with something. Won't your mother miss you?"

"She wanted me to come. It would be pointless to come for just a few weeks. And she's got the other two . . . Wouldn't mind betting you see them before too long."

He was watching my reaction.

"I can cope if it's the English summer. Brothers? Sisters?"

"One of each."

"And what does your father do?"

"He's a lecturer at the local teachers' college. He'll miss me more than Mum will."

"Oh. Why's that?"

Ed shifted uneasily in his chair, as if any kind of personal analysis or dissection was foreign to him.

"Dad's not a happy man. Not too good at his job, not too happy with Mum—it's like he gets nowhere. People don't dislike him, they just . . . don't think much to him. Take him for granted, switch off when he speaks. It's not a real happy home."

"I know all about homes like that."

"Do you? Anyway, he sort of fixes his hopes on me. Carol's Mum's favorite and I'm his."

"At least you have some kind of relationship. What are his hopes for you?"

"Oh, maybe champion athlete—runner, footballer."

"Are you that good?"

"No. To be perfectly honest, I'm not. I'm not built for a footballer. Football to us is what you call Rugby—Rugby League."

"I've dimly heard of it."

"And I'm not quite fast enough to be a champion runner. I suppose the asthma doesn't help."

"Athletes have pretty short careers. It's not a job for life."

Ed looked worldly wise.

"In Australia, sport opens doors. Dad would settle for my being a really successful businessman or a top civil servant. Or even going into politics."

"Politics is pretty dirty in Australia, isn't it?"

"One degree up from the sewage farm."

I smiled.

"We had your man Menzies over here in the war. Seemed to think he ought to be asked to take over the country. We settled for Churchill instead. What about your mother? What does she want for you?"

The boy smiled.

"Oh, anything that would make me famous, paying good money, anything involving a lovely home, beautiful wife, healthy kids. Do you know what she had me christened?"

"Edmund?" I said cunningly.

"Edmund Fearing Clements. She sets great store by the connection with the Old Country. I get it from her, calling England that. And she also calls it 'home,' though she's never been here."

"Hasn't she? Why not?"

"Married too early, I suppose. There's a sense of—I suppose you'd call it frustration in our house."

At least he was opening up. I was pleased.

"So we're related through your mother, are we?"

"That's right. Dad's family have been Aussies for as long as you like, but Mum's always been very conscious that her father was born over here."

"That would be my aunt Clare's son, I suppose. We were never close. I think his name was Leopold."

"Search me. He died when I was about five. It's Mum who has this thing about family. I think you're what you are, not what your ancestors way back were."

Admirable sentiments. But they didn't explain why, a week after docking at Southampton, he turned up on my doorstep, having done a preliminary reconnaissance of Blakemere.

CHAPTER THIRTEEN

TAKING OVER

The great joy of my early womanhood was not love, not "sex," but learning my trade of banker.

You will say this was unnatural, you may even say it was contrary to what you know of my early life, so cynical had I always been of the Fearing Family and its self-worship as one of the world's great banking firms. You may feel that I sold my soul for a mess of financial pottage. I see it quite differently. I was learning to take my place as one of the country's leading bankers, and I was the first woman who would occupy such a position. I am still the only woman who has done so, and I look like remaining the only one for quite a time. I was also one of the few women in the country in any position of great power and responsibility. Even now I am proud of that fact. To the younger me, bright and determined, it was heady stuff.

There again, it was a job of intense interest, particularly to someone with my sort of brain and my interests. It was also extremely complex—a many-layered vocation, which it seemed would take a lifetime to learn. Did I take too long learning it, did I labor over details when I should have intuitively got to its heart? I don't think so. I believe I understood the profession's complications and reverberations, as my grandfather had done, and as I think my father did not. I should say that I don't think I was hindered by people putting obstacles in my way. Oh, they did that all right: women were alien beings to most men in the banking world, particularly the older ones. But the more they tried to thwart me, the more they tried to withhold information or advice they would readily have given to a young man, the more I delighted in finding out and deciding for myself—and perhaps subsequently parading before them the fact that I did not need them or their help. It became a sort of game, a battle. I almost always won.

"Sarah has a man's brain," my father used to say, proudly.

"I'll take that as a compliment," I would say, looking round at whatever the company was that was being boasted to, "but I don't think there are such things as men's or women's brains."

The more competent I became at all aspects of the job, the more my father—I was about to say let go the reins, but it was not quite that. My father got great pleasure out of being Claudius Fearing, the banker—enjoyed *being* Fearing's Bank. But the more I mastered one area of the profession, the more he was inclined to leave that area to me.

"See Sarah about that," he would say to a colleague or underling, without thinking there was anything unusual (or demeaning to him) in the order. "She's the expert on that."

So something of his old dilettante side reasserted itself, and he found he could take life more easily—travel, visit in other great houses, simply relax. Sometimes he would take down a musical comedy star or "Gaiety girl" to Blakemere. It caused no scandal. This was the Edwardian era. The King set the tone, and the King's penchant for actresses who could mix in Society circles was well known. My father's ladies were in the lighter branches of the trade, but Aunt Jane always talked to them as if they were serious artists ("I'm sure the world is waiting for your Juliet"), and at dinner she would question them about what she fondly imagined were the latest trends in contemporary theatre: "Is Mr. Pinero writing another of his controversial pieces?"

It was during the Great War that I strengthened my position at Fearing's Bank, and put the succession beyond question. That was in every way appropriate: with the men away being slaughtered like cattle at the front, women in Britain were learning new skills, taking on heavier labor, finding there were few jobs that absolutely demanded a man's greater strength. When my father was not in London, and sometimes when he was, I was in charge at the Bank's headquarters in Watling Street, and whatever was said by the older functionaries behind my back, my authority was unquestioned to my face.

"It's a completely new world," said my father, both admiring and complaining. "An old buffer like me doesn't feel at home anymore."

The human abatoirs in northern France hit my father very hard. All the younger men he knew seemed to have been taken: clerks from the bank, ingenue young performers from the Doyly Carte, footmen and gardeners and stable lads from Blakemere. For all of them he knew well he shed a tear, until by 1916 the well seemed to have dried up, and when the news of further deaths were brought to him, he just shook his head and went on with his work. My mother's death, soon after the war's end, brought even less reaction from him.

"Will you go to the funeral?" he asked, coming to my office.

"No."

"I thought not. You're quite right. I shan't go myself. The time for these hypocrisies is past. We'll send Jane."

Aunt Jane, he clearly implied, had not outgrown the hypocrisies of the past—and essentially he was right: decent reticence and a covering up of any cause of embarrassment were as much a part of her view of life in 1919 as they had been in 1885. She was most distressed that we both refused to go to the funeral, and the day after my mother was expensively buried (in that respect, at least, we conformed to expectations), she telephoned, greatly daring, to say that she thought of stopping on in Torquay for a few weeks to recoup her strength after the "terrible years" of the War. A few days later, my father wrote to her to tell her that, if she preferred to settle there, that was perfectly all right by both of us, and of course her income was assured.

"Blakemere's days as a great house are numbered," he wrote. "It is now a dinosaur of a building."

Aunt Jane did prefer the gentilities of Torquay to a reduced Blakemere, and she soon got around her a satisfactory circle of acquaintance, for if Blakemere was a house of the past, the name Fearing still counted for something. The air of her little group was heavy with nostalgia for the Old Days—for standards, courteous manners, people who knew their place. Contrariwise there was a bitterness about the war, about Trade Unions, about universal education, and about anything else that was held to be responsible for the passing of the old way of life. Aunt Jane did not have the sort of brain that might have questioned what lay behind the old facade of standards and courtesies.

"Jane has the mind of a suet pudding," said Aunt Sarah, after a visit to her at Torquay. I saw little of Aunt Sarah, but I judged that on balance she had not only the better brain, but had had the better life—quirkiness, oddity, obsessions notwithstanding. I intended to have a better life still.

My father closed down four-fifths of Blakemere after the war. There was no way such a battleship of a house could be staffed in the 1920's. He simply had stairways and corridors boarded up, and had curtains hung over the boards. The trouble was, the rooms we still lived in were the same old large, cold, drafty, intimidating rooms we had always lived in—altogether too ludicrously grand, and no less so with the bulk of the house shut down. Since we had almost never gone into the boarded-up sections, it made very little difference. And the reduced number of servants—a regiment, rather than an army—still cooked and cleaned and ministered to us very much as before.

The end came for my father in 1925. We were by now so close it was almost incredible to think back to my forlorn, unloved state as a child. That was something he never referred to, even when he suspected he had not long to live. He had had a minor heart attack while out shooting, and was brought back to the house by two of the male servants. I think he knew this was only a first warning, and there was more to come. Three evenings later, I sat by his bed, holding his hand in mine, and he said, "I was never involved with the Frank business, Sarah."

I just nodded, and clutched his hand tighter. He had a second, more serious attack during the night, and died alone.

After his day in London, Ed spent a few days around Blakemere. After two nights, he asked me if I wanted him to move on, and I told him he could stay as long as it suited him. I liked having him around. And quite apart from that, I was curious. I wanted to find out who he was.

He made some phone calls the next day to people he had met in London, and talked about the trip they planned to take to poor old war-damaged Europe. He scrupulously left threepence or sixpence by the phone after each call. I quietly accepted them. As my grandfather used to say, without a hint of a smile, "If you're rich, people think you're made of money."

Ed wanted to be of help, he said; he didn't want to "bludge." I gathered from the context this meant he wanted to pay his way by doing something useful. He didn't want suggestions, however, and in his roamings around Blakemere with the dogs he decided he wanted to cut the lawns, to see how the house would have looked in its heyday. I wasn't at all sure this could be categorized as useful. I had had practically nothing done in the Blakemere grounds since September 1939, and I saw no reason to now.

"The grass is practically waist high," I said. "You'll have to get at it with a scythe before you can use the mowers."

"A scythe? I've never used one of those."

"Nobody much does these days. I'll see if I can find one in the stables."

I certainly couldn't use a scythe myself, but when I had disentangled one from a heap of old garden implements, and when he had sharpened it with a whetstone, I could demonstrate the sort of movements that I had seen the gardeners and farm laborers use with them in the days of my childhood.

"I'll soon get the hang," said Ed, cheerfully. And he did. When I went back at midday with a packet of sandwiches, most of the croquet lawn was down to manageable height, and he was about to get working on the great lawn beside the Terrace.

"It's a piece of cake once you've got the knack," he said, sitting down beside me.

"I can't afford any fuel for the motor mowers, I'm afraid," I said. "If you want them looking as they used to look it'll have to be the hand mowers or nothing."

"She'll be right. I've nothing else to do."

"You should be traveling around, seeing the country."

"You soon get indigestion if you do nothing but that. You have to have periods in between when you just relax—give the eyes and the mind a rest."

"I suppose that's sensible," I admitted. "I never went much on sightseeing myself."

"You must have seen the world—done the Grand Tour and all that."

"I started one, but it was truncated: I got bored."

"Bored? With so much to see?"

"I'm afraid so."

"Don't you like Europe?"

"I've nothing against it. Before the war I used to go to Paris, Brussels, Amsterdam—just for a few days. To eat well, in Paris to go to the theater, the Opéra. To tell you the truth, I was always glad to get home, and back to work."

"I suppose if you've got this"—Ed waved his hand at the brooding mass of the boarded-up Blakemere—"you wouldn't want to sightsee at other grand places."

"Possibly having *this*, as you call it, may have made me a bit skeptical or cynical about 'grand places'."

He paused in his munching of his egg-and-cress sandwich and looked at me. His face is individual, but rather attractive, perched on the top of his beanpole body. When that fills out, he will break hearts.

"Will you show me round?" he said suddenly.

I shot him a glance, I think a suspicious one.

"Blakemere?. . . . I can't unboard the place, you know."

"Of course not."

"Why do you want to see it?"

"I don't know. We have rich people in Australia, but this is something . . . something way out of our line."

"Well, I suppose since I had the power turned off, I can turn it on again, for an hour or two. I've got the main door keys at the gatehouse . . ." I felt I had to warn him. "But it's a terrible barn of a place, you know. Everything overdone: too grand, pretentious, heavy. There was no judgment went into it. Money, but no judgment. Much of it is laughable, in dreadful taste."

"I don't suppose I have good taste myself."

I shrugged. "Admittedly taste changes from generation to generation. But I don't think Blakemere will ever be admired. In fact, I imagine that in a few years it will be a ruin."

"All the more reason to see it now. It's part of my family background. And even if some of it is in terrible taste, it has—I can see from the outside—one thing that you never get in Australia."

"What's that?"

"Splendor."

It was only a week or two after my father's death that I heard rumors that Bankside School was in difficulties, or at any rate going through a bad patch. I was in the thick of taking over—not of taking over the Bank, where most things had been in my hands for some time, but in taking over Blakemere. Even with a reduced staff, with the shutting off of so much of the place and the decision to let most of the land revert to pasture, there was still much to be done, and it was labor without love. I didn't think "why me?" where the Bank was concerned, but I did very much think it where Blakemere was concerned. I decided to take an afternoon off, and drive into Wentwood to talk to Edith and Robert.

I took Richard with me—he was then in the last year of his life. I have not said much about Richard, because there is not much to say. He had grown but he had not grown up. He was the same loving, simple, rather lethargic person he had always been, and I loved him as I loved no one else. He was my link with the past. His day-to-day existence had been transformed by a bright idea in the first year of the war, when he had been given a piece of kitchen garden all his own. Tending it, growing vegetables, lavishing on them all the love he had left over from his small circle of loved ones, became his existence, and a very joyful one it was. He readily agreed to come to Wentwood, though, because Edith and Robert, who both treated him with a brisk and unsentimental affection, had always been among his favorite people.

I let myself be chauffeur-driven. I drove myself as a rule, and with great pleasure, but so soon after the funeral, in deep mourning, it seemed right to have a chauffeur take us. What odd ideas we had, only twenty years ago, and how the hypocrisies my father spoke of did cling on!

We all had tea and cakes together, after I had been welcomed at the door by Robert and had looked around a bit, wondering whether the place had outlived its time. When we had eaten (and Edith and Robert always did themselves very nicely in the food line), Robert took Richard off to the gardens, and to watch the girls playing tennis. Robert always realized that Edith and I went so far back we liked to talk alone.

Edith's hair was gray now, her figure firm but substantial, and she looked like—was probably seen by the girls as—a typical mid-Victorian headmistress. How very untypical she was, I was one of the few to know, though I'm sure her husband's job before marriage was still the subject of whisperings in Wentwood.

"You'll be thinking of selling the school and retiring soon, I suppose," I said.

"I will *not!*" said Edith, in her most emphatic voice. "What would we do? One thing about owning your own school is that no one can tell you when you have to retire."

"Is the school doing well?"

Her eyes glinted. Edith was never easily fooled. She certainly always saw through me.

"Not as well as it used to do. I suppose you've heard that?"

"Yes. I wondered as I came through: is the problem that you're starting to seem old-fashioned?"

"It is, partly. We're *not* old fashioned, not in the things that matter. What we teach, how we teach it, is bang up-to-date, and we've several young and enthusiastic teachers here. But we *look* frowsty and Victorian."

"People are so silly, judging by look."

"When we started up we had to be absolutely strict, the proprieties personified." She looked at me straight, her way when talking around something we would do best not to talk about openly. "Because of my marriage nothing else would do. Well, we're modifying the school uniform, we're having a complete redecoration of the schoolrooms and the dormitories. But it takes time before the general public becomes conscious of these things."

"Do you want to advertise?"

"Advertise, yes. But also to pick out the potential parents—I know this town through and through, know all the families with girls of the right age—and write them individual letters, stressing that we unite a modern syllabus with traditional standards and strict codes of behavior. It will be what a lot of them will want. I really do believe it will work."

"Do you want a loan? Would a thousand pounds help?"

She shook her head. "Five hundred would be more than enough. And it would be a loan—with appropriate interest."

"I don't take interest from my friends. You were a lifeline to me when I had practically no one else."

"I'm a poor friend to you now. We've hardly said anything about your father's death. You must feel awfully alone, over there in that barn of a place."

"Not much more than before," I said, making light of what she said, though it was true. "You know, my father and I had got to be quite close over the last twenty years or so, but it's more like losing a valued and trusted colleague than a father."

"Yes. That sounds odd, but I can understand it."

"He'd had the attack two days earlier, and that was a warning. He knew he might not have long. . . . Do you know what he said to me before he died?"

"No."

Was I wrong in suspecting an access of tension in her body?

"He said: 'I was never involved in that Frank business.' "

"I expect that will be the business of your uncle Frank's marriage." Edith was making a patent effort to make her voice sound even and everyday. "That was a disaster, wasn't it? And he didn't have anything to do with it, so far as we heard in the schoolroom. It's no wonder he would want to dissociate himself from it, though."

I left a second's silence.

" 'That Frank business' doesn't sound like marriage to me. It sounds like something even more disastrous. Frank disappeared off the face of the earth, Edith."

"Now you're sounding like a little girl again, Sarah. He did nothing of the sort. He went to settle in Australia."

I felt it unworthy of her to peddle the old family lie.

"And nothing has been heard of him since," I said drily. Unwisely I waded straight in. "Robert knows what happened on that night, Edith."

"He does nothing of the sort!"

"And if he knows, you know."

Edith stood up, her face red with anger.

"Sarah, I'm surprised at you—no, not surprised, shocked. I didn't think you would catch your family's disease of thinking people can be bought."

"I didn't mean—"

"Oh, but you did. You come here offering a loan, and you think we'll then have to supply you with information that you imagine we have. And you're quite wrong, Sarah. You may have a banker's head, but you have a novel-reader's imagination. I blame myself. You were an adolescent when your uncle Frank left Blakemere, and you conceived all manner of nonsenses to account for it, drawn from the sort of books we used to read. Your uncle Frank is in Australia, unless he has died there. Now I think you had better go. We will survive without your money, and it will be better for us to do so."

There was nothing for it but to collect Richard—who sensed there was something wrong, as Robert did, too—and be driven home. It was very quiet in the car. I was deep in thought, and Richard kept looking at me nervously. For someone who was never blamed, he was strangely anxious when he imagined he might have done something wrong.

I acquitted myself of trying to buy Edith's secret. I would have offered her a loan in any case. But then my logical brain said to me: but you did *use* the offer of a loan to try to make her break her silence, didn't you? And of that I could not acquit myself.

The next day I wrote her a note:

Dear Edith,

I am profoundly sorry for what happened. Please can we meet in the future as if nothing has changed?

Your loving friend,
Sarah

And we did meet, and met often, and nothing more was said between us. Edith and Robert managed to fund their campaign to woo back parents by private retrenchment, and the campaign worked. I think that gave Edith if not her husband more satisfaction than accepting a loan from me.

Nevertheless, when the anger had evaporated, when I had examined my motives and found them less than entirely pure, still some facts remained. There was no reason for Edith's anger unless she and Robert did indeed have information about the death of Uncle Frank. For a time it struck me as incomprehensible, even absurd, that she should want to deny it to me, so close to her, and so long after the event. Only after mature reflection did I realize that she had to deny all knowledge of events that could have led to a much-loved husband being charged as an accessory after the fact to a murder.

CHAPTER FOURTEEN

Reopening

The day after Ed made his surprising request I had to make a brief trip to London—to Whitehall and to the Bank. I had a long talk to Digby Fearing, my stand-in, and when I told him I was going to reopen Blakemere for a few hours, to show it to an Australian cousin, and asked him if he wanted to be part of the expeditionary force, he said, "Good heavens, no. It was bad enough going there as a child, without going back to it all dusty and boarded up."

"You hated it, did you?"

"Of course. How else could a strange child feel—so enormous a place, and so intimidating? I hardly dared utter a word the entire time I was there. I suppose it was different for you, being brought up there."

"I hated it, too."

"Or thought you did. You never made any attempt to get rid of it after it came to you."

"I've never been one for lost causes."

"Who's the Australian cousin? One of Clare's brood?"

"I think so. He's rather vague. Was it Leopold, Clare's son who had to disappear rather suddenly to Australia?"

"That's right. Named after one of Queen Victoria's sons. It never got his father any royal commissions that I know of. Leopold was a charming young man, but just . . . lacking something."

At least this boy hasn't tried to off-load bogus share certificates on me.

"Honesty," I supplied. "Well, if you don't want to see Blakemere again . . ."

But for some reason—not at all because I was afraid of him—I didn't want to go into the old house alone with Ed. I wanted someone with me who knew the place in the old days, perhaps as a sort of buffer (or maybe I mean blotting paper, or even conductor) for my memories and emotions. It was the instinct of confronting my past not on my own, or with someone who could never understand, but with someone who knew something about it and would feel with me. In the end I rang Gabriel South, Bea's son, the Labour Party agent in Bedford, and he readily agreed.

"It'll be a bit like exploring a prehistoric cave," he said. "Something from quite another age."

That about summed it up.

Ed was going to Yorkshire for a few days, and we arranged it for the day after his return. Gabriel is a bright, bustling personality—a keen brain, but someone who has never lost the common touch. He and Ed got on at once. After lunch we equipped ourselves with the enormous key ring and with powerful torches, and I took the Morris and parked it just beside the stone steps leading up to the Grand Entrance.

"We'll have enough walking to do once we get inside,"I said, a touch grimly.

I paused at the top of the steps, surveying the sadly overgrown gardens and lawns at the house's front. Then I selected the right key. Gabriel did not offer to open the door, sensing this was a symbolic moment. I put the key in the lock of the great oaken door, and it turned—without difficulty, but with an enormous clang, as it always had when Mr. McKay opened it early in the morning. Gabriel helped me to push the dead weight of door, unoiled for seven years, and I gestured to Ed to unbolt and swing open its pair. It was a sunny summer's day, but the warm light barely penetrated beyond the threshold. We looked at each other, Gabriel and me, and then we all crossed into the Grand Entrance Hall. I flashed my torch around it first on the walls at eye level, then gradually up to the ceiling.

"Jesus *Christ*!" said Ed. And then: "Sorry!"

"That's the main staircase," I said, flashing the torch up and down its magnificent expanse. "There are others, of course. I used to wait up there, peering through the marble balustrade, hoping that my favorite uncle would be coming home . . ." I put the memories from me briskly. "Now, the main power points are just outside the door to the kitchens, Gabriel."

"I remember." We tracked down a long corridor, intensely gloomy but not frightening, until I could flash my torch at the series of boxes. "I'll do it," Gabriel said, "but I'll need a chair or a ladder."

We got a chair from the family dining room nearby—an upright chair, inevitably gilded but covered in sheeting. Gabriel stood on it and pulled a series of levers. Then I went over to the nearest light switch.

"There!" I said. A dim light came on, less than a revelation. I began to trek around, and Gabriel did the same—down corridors, into the dining room, into other rooms, bringing with every switch more and more light on the dusty scene. "There! There! There!" we said.

Ed said nothing. He walked around as if in a dream. We went back to the Grand Entrance Hall and he stood there, head tilted back, eyes scanning the painted ceiling way above him. We went on to the drawing rooms, then the Salon, the family rooms, the Great Dining Hall where Mr. Gladstone had sealed my fate, on, on, on, through all the grandiose fantasies of one of the Victorian age's least imaginative architects. All the furniture was swathed in sheeting, and some of the pictures (those few with any artistic worth had been removed to storage), but everywhere Ed looked his eyes widened with wonder at the ornate decoration, the miniatory classical figures in the ceilings, the hideous knobbly clocks, the tormented table legs protruding from under the dust sheets. Dust—dust everywhere, the dust of wartime years covering and dulling everything.

"It's incredible!" Ed said at last.

"It is that," I agreed.

"Wonderful! Just wonderful!"

I looked at Gabriel and we both raised our eyebrows.

When I had absorbed Edith's rebuke, and decided it was stinging, partly deserved, yet also self-protective on her part, I did what was customary with me: I began to reassert my control of the situation. I am not bossy, I do not enjoy putting people in their places or rubbing their noses in my superior wealth or position, but I do not like feeling at a disadvantage, and I do like to know precisely where I stand so I will never be at a loss. At times I can use surreptitious means to this end, even be devious and underhand. I was, and had to be, a secretive child.

Something had to be done. I had to know. If not what happened, then who was involved. But I had to be sly, had to tell no one what I was up to. The skeletons in the family cupboard might be too frightening even for me. I had to proceed still, as I had always preferred to, deviously.

I called in Digby Fearing, already a power in the Bank's central office, and asked him for a complete list of the Bank and the Family's pensioners and debtors, omitting only those who were exclusively connected to the Bank itself. I wanted servants and connections, people who had worked at Blakemere, people who were associated with Uncle Frank and his end.

When I got the list, and the details of the sums involved, it was quite easy to pick out the people who were of interest, though it was also nostalgic to go through the long list of Blakemere staff, men and women whose names I had to recall with effort, and see how they were rewarded on retirement and how long they lived to remain on our list of pensioners. They were rewarded well, even generously, but I wouldn't want to suggest that the Fearings were lavish with their money. Rich people who want to stay rich never are.

Some names stood out at once. Joe Mossman, though never head gardener or in any sort of position of responsibility among the outdoor staff, was given three times the normal gratuity on retirement, and his pension was continued after his death to his married daughter until her death. Joe was old, and very loyal, when I knew him. He was one of the figures I thought I had seen from my bedroom window on the night of the burial. Presumably it was thought he might have talked to his daughter in his dotage, and her silence was also bought. A precisely similar arrangement was come to over Ben Burke: he had been pensioned off in 1892, but the arrangement was changed in 1893: the gratuity was added to, and his pension was continued after his death, first to his wife, then to his son.

I read with particular interest the section relating to Robert and Edith. It was much simpler. As long as they remained in service at Blakemere there was no record of any payment (though it may well be that one went to Robert). When they married and set up their school in Wentwood, they were given a lump-sum payment of four thousand pounds. I suspect that this arrangement may have been at Edith's insistence, even if it was Robert who negotiated it. By accepting a regular payment they would have become pensioners of the Fearing family. The lump sum meant that the connection was, at least financially, at an end, and they were now on their own. I felt sure she preferred it that way.

The only non-family members to figure in the fateful family conference were the Coverdales—and Mary was, of course, by then technically a Fearing. What I took to be her pensioning-off and silence-buying was paid to her father, and ceased at his death—presumably because she herself was also dead by then. It was the sum of fifteen hundred a year—a decidedly generous sum by the standards of the time.

What was to be done with such a record of people long dead, whose descendants, even, were dead? I stewed over it, I remember, for a weekend, but in the end I came to the conclusion that Robert and Edith were the only people on the list that I could approach. Shame should have stopped me, and fear of losing one of my best and oldest friends. Yet I felt overwhelming curiosity, felt I *had* to know. My mind tugging me in two, at least, directions, I went and had tea with her again, determined to bring up the matter one more time. But when, in a moment of silence as she poured second cups I said "Edith—" there must have been something in my voice that warned her, and she fixed me with an eye that was filled with the sort of sternness she had seldom had used on me even in the schoolroom.

"Yes, Sarah?" she said, her voice the hardest steel. She knew me through and through, perhaps the only person who did.

"I am awfully glad things have come right with the school," I said, feebly.

The list went into a desk drawer and gathered dust.

"Dust!" said Gabriel South, in one of the big bedrooms. "Dust everywhere. Mortality, the past, death."

Ed was more interested in the life that had once been there.

"Whose room was this?" he asked.

"No one's in particular," I said, memories crowding in. "Used occasionally for an important guest. But it's the one my cousin Richard was born in. He was retarded, and I loved him very much. So did all the South children."

"We did," agreed Gabriel. "He was a lovely person."

"Yes—he seemed to lead a charmed life. Even his death seemed to come without fuss—a cold, influenza, then just snuffed out. I was desolate, but somehow it seemed right. I always saw Richard as an innocent, untouched by all the guilt that afflicted us, and the angst and competitiveness and frustration."

"Speak for yourself," said Gabriel. "I don't remember being afflicted by any of those things."

"I meant the Fearings, of course. It was after Richard's death that I decided to open Blakemere to the public. I wouldn't have wanted him to become some sort of sideshow."

"Will you open it again, when things get back to normal?" asked Ed.

"Not me. I've got much too much to do. Opening a place like this to the public is a full-time job, like being director of a big museum. I've sometimes wondered whether I could get rid of it to the National Trust or some such body."

"Oh, no!" said Ed.

"Before they'd accept they'd want a hefty wad of endowment money with it," said Gabriel.

"Jeez!" said Ed. "You mean that you'd have to pay them before they'd even accept it as a gift?"

"That's perfectly reasonable," I pointed out. "Think of the maintenance and the repair work. If I'm not willing to undertake them, as a rich woman, why should the Trust let me unload the burden on to them?"

"But if you *gave* them this place?"

I had to explain the financial facts of life to him patiently.

"It's a white elephant, Ed. It has and can have no useful purpose. If it were a hospital, the drafts and cold would kill patients off in no time. A monster lunatic asylum? Even the modern world hasn't produced potential patients in such large numbers. It's outlived any purpose it once had."

"But if it were opened to the public, wouldn't the revenue—?"

"No," I said. "It wouldn't."

I opened Blakemere to the public in 1932. That gave me the opportunity to reverse my father's decision to shut off large parts of the house—a quite unsuccessful attempt to reduce it to a more human scale. Not, of course, that I intended to admit the public to the whole house—we would have had to issue three-day tickets, and institute a rescue service for lost visitors—but the boarding-up presented a most unattractive appearance and gave a misleading impression of the place.

I tried my own solution to the size problem. I removed my living quarters to four rooms in the most modest section of the house—on the second floor, under the attics and two floors up from the kitchens. These rooms had not been used, I suspected, more than five or six times in the house's history. Then they would have been occupied by the family's least-valued houseparty guests. The fact that they were over the kitchen had disadvantages where smell was concerned, but advantages where the freshness and hotness of meals was concerned—much more to the point, I felt. I ate frugally, but the dishes were brought up an obscure back staircase by one of the much-reduced kitchen staff, and when she took the silver covers off the plates, steam arose. So here I made my home, and tried to be cozy, well away from the visitors to our fadingly magnificent main rooms.

Nineteen thirty-two, at the height of the Depression, was hardly an auspicious time to be opening to the public. Initially the opening was every weekend during the summer months, and curiosity ensured that the first weekends saw a steady stream of visitors—some from the nearest big cities, but mostly local people anxious to view a house—or palace—which had loomed large on the physical horizon of Buckinghamshire and on the mental landscape of their lives. These locals often gazed with awe at the sheer size, lavishness, and overstuffed nature of the place.

More sophisticated visitors looked with a more cynical eye. Mingling with the public, I gradually got the sense that they were seeing the place as slightly comic: it was a memorial to a family that had had a ludicrously overblown sense of its own importance and its place in the national pantheon. I heard sniggers. There were satirical pars in newspapers. Gradually, as the years of the thirties passed, Blakemere began to assume, in a minor way, the status of a national joke.

That made me feel a lot better about the place. But the admission charges never brought me in enough to pay for the necessary attendants to oversee the operation. The place was a joke, but among a small coterie. Blakemere open to the public operated at a greater loss than Blakemere reserved for family and friends.

The attitude taken to Blakemere by thirties sophisticates was not one that Ed would have understood. But then, he is young, and colonial. If, as he said, splendor is not something Australia encompasses, how could he have learned to distinguish bogus from true splendor?

"It's just . . . overpowering," he said, as we ended our tour. And neither Gabriel nor I would quarrel with that.

"Do you want to go round again on your own?" I asked. He nodded, wide-eyed still. "Well, go on. If you find anything pocketable that you want as a souvenir, just take it."

He nodded happily, then his face fell.

"I suppose that means that this is a once-in-a lifetime experience, and I'm never going to see the place properly opened up?"

"Yes—I think I can promise you that you won't."

He shook his head sadly, but he went off, doubly determined to absorb and fix in his memory as much as he could of this wonderful place. Gabriel and I shook our heads at his naive enthusiasm, then we went to the Great Entrance Hall and sat on the bottom step of the staircase.

"Should you have told him to take something?" he asked.

"The temptation would have been irresistible anyway. That's not thieving, that's souvenir-hunting. You know there's nothing here I value."

Then we put the house out of our minds and got on to Labour Party business. It was quite a while before Ed came back, and when he did he stood for some minutes in the Hall, looking up, around and down, taking it in, making it part of his mental landscape. Though I thought he was misguided, I liked him for it. Enthusiasm is always attractive. At last he tore himself away from the sights and came over.

"It's been the experience of a lifetime," he said. "I want to thank you, but I can't find the right words."

"I've quite enjoyed seeing the old place," I said briskly, getting up.

"Oh, by the way, I took this," he said, pulling something out of his pocket. It was a corkscrew in the typical Blakemere style, with a large knobbly handle of pure silver.

"You're welcome to it," I said. "Where was it?"

"Back of a drawer in . . . well, I'm not sure what: one of the drawing rooms, I reckon."

"Well, I wish you luck of it, and plenty of good bottles to use it on. Now let's go out into the sunlight. I think I shall feel like Lord Carnarvon emerging from the tomb of Tutankhamen. Let's go and turn off the lights."

That done, and the place restored to decent darkness, we made a torchlight procession to the Great Entrance Hall. We went out through the main door, and I turned to lock it. The heavy clanking sounded symbolically final to me. It was still a bright, not-too-warm sunlight outside, and the rolling countryside looked green and inviting. We walked down the broad steps and got into the car. Ed was very quiet.

"Well, it was interesting to see the old place again," said Gabriel, cheerful but unawed. "That's where my mother became the sort of person she was."

"Yes, it was," I agreed. "She was the first person who was kind to me. The old place must have taught her something good."

"Was your mother a Fearing?" Ed asked Gabriel.

He laughed. "No. She was a sort of upper-parlormaid here. I don't know the technical title."

"She is part of my earliest memories here," I said. "She was with me when I talked to Mr. Gladstone."

"*Mr. Gladstone*!" almost shouted Ed.

"Yes. I was a little girl, and I was taken to see him at the very grand dinner we were giving for him. He beckoned to me to go over and was nice to me in his way."

Ed subsided into silence. It was as if I'd said I'd talked to Napoleon Bonaparte or Alexander the Great.

When we got back to the gatehouse I put on the kettle for tea, and began buttering some scones. There had been a letter for Ed in the afternoon post, but he just put it in his pocket and wandered round in a dream, sometimes going outside and looking toward Blakemere, then wandering back in but not settling down to anything. Looking into his face, I understood for the first time the word "moonstruck."

"I still can't take it in," he said.

"I can see that," I said. "Blakemere's a house that's difficult to digest."

"You're so *cynical* about it," he protested.

"You would be if you'd lived in it for long," said Gabriel, coming to my defense. "It's just a filthy-rich Victorian banker's folly."

"*Just*!" came back Ed. "There's no *just* about that place."

And there at least he was right. Blakemere is the filthy-rich Victorian banker's folly magnified to the nth degree. Over tea and scones Ed showed he was still in his dream world.

"Now the war's over and things are getting back to normal," he said in a faraway voice, "you could open up the house, have house-parties again. People motoring down for the weekend, playing tennis and croquet. You say there's a golf course out there somewhere. You could have it restored. You could have parties—I bet there's wonderful wine in the cellars, isn't there? People will want to have fun again, like in the twenties. And you could host political gatherings. The politicians of all parties, getting together to solve the nation's problems. And international ones, too. You'd be the ideal person to be hostess, spanning both groups. You'd be good at bringing people together, too. You've certainly made me feel at home."

He faded into grateful silence.

"To take your first point," said Gabriel, "the war is over, but things are not getting back to normal."

"No they're not," I said, in agreement. "And perhaps you'll tell me where I'm going to find the gardeners and the greensmen, the chefs and the footmen, the parlormaids and the skivvies. They were difficult to find between the wars; now they'd be impossible. They don't exist anymore, and they'll never come back. The world has changed. People have done war work now, and been properly paid for it, so even in the rural districts they're not going back to being slave laborers at slave rates on the farms and big estates."

Ed looked down into his lap, so I added: "You'll understand when you've been in Britain longer."

As I got up to refresh the teapot he leaned forward for a scone, and felt his letter crinkle in his pocket. He took out an airmail envelope and slitted it open with a table knife. When I got back from the kitchen he was deep in his letter.

"Who's it from?" I asked.

"My father," he mumbled. "Whingeing on. Says he and Mum are having rows. Tell me something new." He read through to the end, then slipped it back into his pocket. "Anyway, he's solved the question of who I am."

"Who you are?"

"I mean who I am in the Fearing clan. He says that Mum's father was Frank Fearing. Suppose if you knew Mr. Gladstone you must have known him."

CHAPTER FIFTEEN

Ed and I

I will not seek to justify what I did next. I will just tell you what it was. You are by now in a position to make your own judgments of me.

The following morning, when Ed had gone on a hiking excursion on public footpaths in the direction of Northampton, I went up to his room. I was glad I didn't need to rummage through his baggage to find the letter from his father. It was on his bedside table, together with his reading matter, *Lost Horizon*, by James Hilton. I opened the letter, put on my reading glasses, and scanned it. It was closely typed on an old and dirty typewriter, and it made the most of every square inch of the sheet of wafer-thin paper.

"Dear Ed," it began,

> Glad to have an address to write to, and your mum's glad she knows how to get in touch. The cold weather doesn't suit your mother, chilblains as usual, the girls have copped it. Me too!. . . " [I omit here a lot of domestic moans.] "Things are changing out here, Ed. The servicemen are coming home, we've got a lot of them at the College. They've done a lot for the Country, no doubt about that Ed, but they are older and

have their own ideas after serving overseas many of them so they are not easy to teach. As usual I seem to get all the Bolshie ones, just my luck." [I omit a lot of professional whingeing, to adopt Ed's lovely word.] "It was good to hear you and Miss Sarah Fearing are getting on like a house on fire. She is an influential person, quite apart from being a fabulously rich one. I always said to your mum that she ought to make contact with her family, but she accused me of wanting their money, which is daft, but if you've got rich people closely related to you it doesn't make sense to ignore them does it. [I was beginning to hope that Ed's father did not teach English at that Teachers' College of his. If he did, I had every sympathy with his Bolshie ex-serviceman students.] So what I say is, get well in there, Ed. It can't be bad, can it. And if she's a nice woman like you say it would be a real leg up for you. I think you ought to make a long stay over there now you are there. Would send money but it's scarce—you know how it is.

Your loving
Dad

I folded up the crisp paper. I was beginning to get a rather vivid picture in my mind of Ed's dad, and I didn't like it much. Mind you, to be fair to Ed, I had the impression that he didn't like him much, either.

I was about to put the letter back in precisely the position it had been in on his bedside table when I realized I had not found what I had been looking for. I read the letter through carefully again: nothing about the name of Ed's grandfather. I was puzzled. If it was not in the letter, why had he only brought it out after reading it? Then I suddenly saw a note on the back of the envelope, beside the boy's home address in Bathurst. It was a scrawled note in immature handwriting, and it read:

Tell your cousin your grandfather's name was Frank Fearing.

I put the letter back on the little table and went about my work.

But as I did so, I thought. The note seemed to be in response to a query in a letter from Ed—perhaps one that arrived after his father's letter had been written and sealed, perhaps one only remembered after it had been. Probably the former, I thought, since his father obviously set great store by "getting well in" with me. On reflection I realized there was an ambiguity in the note: "Tell your cousin your grandfather's name was Frank Fearing" was decidedly different from saying, "Your grandfather's name was Frank Fearing." I mulled over this for some time.

But as I faced the conundrum in intervals of going over Foreign Office papers, I began to see it differently. First of all, I did not get the impression that Ed's dad was the sort of person who would have scrupled to tell a lie. Morally grubby was how I would describe him, on the basis of Ed's description and the letter. The distinction between the two formulas was one that would have been relevant if he was morally finicky, but not if he was morally opaque. Still, the question remained, however he chose to say it: was the claim that Ed's maternal grandfather was Frank Fearing true or false? That I had no means of judging. The only fact that I had that might be relevant was that Ed had pretty obviously not been primed up with the facts of his ancestry before he set out. I pondered the implications of this, and after a time a further possibility occurred to me: that scrawled postscript could be the result of a late-arriving letter from his son *asking* him to say that his grandfather was called Frank Fearing. I ran over all our conversations about the family in my mind: could I have given away to Ed my very special feelings toward my uncle Frank?

I didn't start cooking dinner till Ed arrived back, brown and sweaty but apparently happy, in the gathering twilight. I had by now procured a ration book for him, but to an Australian appetite the portions were tiny, and the lack of choice dreary. He never said anything, but I had the impression he didn't care for liver, but liver is what we had. I made up for it with a wildly extravagant cheese soufflé, made with the eggs from our hens and the mousetrap cheese which is all we can get at the local grocer's—practically all one can get *any* where. Fortunately it rose like a bird, and was light and scrumptious.

"How did you learn to cook?" Ed asked, licking his spoon, always the best compliment.

"I got myself a book at the beginning of the war, when I moved down to this place," I said, remembering. "And of course there are lots of women around here, old kitchen staff at Blakemere, willing to teach me and give me a hand when necessary. Then when I started working at—somewhere I can't talk about—I was completely on my own and it was a matter of trial and error."

"Why can't you talk about this place?"

"Still hush-hush. Code-breaking and suchlike. It was very flattering to be recruited. If I was a private person now I might be cynical about the ban on talking about it, now the war is over, but in my job I can't afford to be. And then, the question is: is the war over?"

Ed nodded wisely, but I rather suspected he knew little or nothing about international affairs. He always gives me the impression that the only ties Australians are willing to acknowledge are with the Mother Country.

"Anyway, you learned," he said.

"Yes, I learned. Though trial and error is a bit painful when you're living on tiny rations," I added ruefully.

"My mum couldn't do anything like this," he said, gesturing to the soufflé dish.

"Hardly the sort of thing the mother of a good-sized family is likely to go in for," I said. "Tell me about your mother."

He had given me the opening I had wanted. I didn't intend the talk to end with his mother.

"Mum? Oh, we just about rub along, but no more. If I try and be fair I can see that she's plenty to grumble about: she married a no-hoper, then got trapped with three children—end of story. What has she to look forward to when we grow up and escape the nest? No life, no outside interests. Dad had a job in a local school, wasn't much of a teacher, got the job at the Teachers' College through having contacts. In these small towns in Australia it's the people you know. . . . But at least he has a job, and quite a good one. Mum just sits at home and cooks the meals. I can see why it's not enough."

"What was her background?"

"Oh, brought up on a property fifty miles out of town."

"A property?"

"Local sheep station—quite a small one. Not particularly prosperous—just about survived the Depression. But being from a sheep property gives you a certain prestige."

"I see."

"Grandma didn't help. I remember her quite well—she died just before the war, not that old. Nice woman, sense of fun, but a bit of a stickler. She was from Geelong, and felt rather superior to New South Wales people. Always insisted on good table manners, on being respectfully spoken to. Dad sometimes whispered that she had *had* to get married—I think that was his revenge for her snootiness."

"Pregnant?"

"Yeah. There's a wedding photograph in our front room. If Mum's not there, Dad will say: 'Taken late 1897; your mother was born March 1898.' If you don't know, it doesn't show; but if you look real close it sets you thinking. Not that it's earth-shattering fifty years on, but Dad likes his little dig."

I made a concession, and went along with the presumption of his grandfather's identity.

"My uncle Frank was said to have one or two by-blows in this area. It's not something I've ever been into. Start to make inquiries and they might be on your doorstep demanding handouts."

Ed grinned. "I'm surprised they don't anyway."

"Knowing my family they probably paid the mothers lump sums and made them sign some absolutely binding declaration forswearing any further claims on the Fearing family. . . . Does your mother make a big thing about being one of the Fearings by birth?"

He shuffled in his seat. His height made it a long shuffle.

"No. . . . Tell you the truth, I don't think it would mean much in Australia. I don't suppose most people would have heard of Fearing's Bank."

"That puts us in our place. I should have thought of that. Did your mother tell you to make contact with me?"

We were straying near to doubtful territory. Ed again showed incipient embarrassment.

"No. It was more my father. My mother just shrugged and said, 'Can't do any harm. Don't expect them to part with any of their money, though. Dad never got anything out of them.' And by the way, I don't expect you to part with any of your money. It's the last thing on my mind."

"Good," I said. "Rich people never part with it readily." But what he had said had interested me. "I suppose your mother resented her father having to struggle through the Depression without support from his family back home?"

"Maybe." He shrugged. "It was my grandmother who pulled the place through those years. He was a lot older than her, of course, and tired. She shouldered the burden, from all I've heard."

"You don't remember your grandfather much, you said?"

"Hardly at all: sitting on his knee and pulling at this gray beard; and a vague feeling that he was a joker, someone who laughed a lot. He died when I was five, I think."

Around 1930, then. My uncle Frank was born in the mid-1850's. So a good long life—if it was his. A thought struck me.

"But your mother didn't inherit the . . . property."

"Good Lord, no. She'd have been hopeless at running it. It's not woman's work, for all my grandmother took to it so well. Though my dad would have been still worse. No, it naturally went to my uncle Jack, her younger brother. He'd helped his mother, and took it over after her death. He's still running it. We don't see much of him. He doesn't get on with my dad—or my mum, particularly. He's a real outback character—tanned and wrinkled and slow, and full of dry jokes. Has a big family—five sons and three daughters."

Sons! Male Fearings! What the family had demanded of Frank, hidden away in the Australian bush. If Grandpapa had not changed his will just before he died they would have been—if legitimate—heirs to Blakemere and to Fearing's Bank. Unless of course their father was Clare's Leopold under a false name, or another of her brood escaping from a cloud in the Old Country. The more I thought of it, the more likely it seemed that the explanation lay there. One could see a son of Leopold's being a bit of a joker, and fathering a large family. Though he would have to have escaped the family curse of unreliability and general hopelessness.

Later that evening, before we went to bed, we made a hot milky drink for ourselves. Ed liked them, and it made me feel I was back in the nursery again. I sat on the sofa in my dressing gown, cradling a large breakfast cup in my hand. Ed sat on the floor at my feet, his long legs forming an upside-down V in front of him. It was oddly comforting to have male company—*young* male company, and for that reason unthreatening. The fact that he had such a nice face, and an eye that seemed to have escaped the calculation that was almost endemic with the Fearings, helped a lot.

"You've got to believe I'm not after a handout from the Fearing millions," he said awkwardly, after there had been pleasant silence between us for some time.

"I do," I said without hesitation. "The Fearing millions, by the way, are much depleted by the war. They'll pick up again, but it will take time—a decade at least, I would guess. I expect I'll be off the active list before things are really back to normal, if they ever are."

He nodded. "The real reason I wanted to make contact was because I wanted to feel I had a family back here, 'home' as mother calls it. It's been hell in Australia during the war years."

I had heard this from Australians before, and I wasn't having any of it.

"From all I've heard you did extremely well, those who didn't serve in the forces: plenty of food, not an enemy in sight, everything pretty much as normal. You seem to work up a submarine being sighted off Sydney Harbor as a threat of invasion and occupation."

My briskness sent him backtracking.

"Yes, of course it was nothing like here—no blitz, no rationing, no V2's. I was exaggerating. But I just mean that if you're growing up in Australia it's important that the Old Country is *there*—that you can dream of paying it a visit, look up family and friends, go to all the things it does well—plays, Prom concerts, lovely homes. And then the war cut all that off. Suddenly we felt so *remote*. A big, undefendable British island at the far end of Asia. And a place where nothing happened—where the highlights would be a footie game on Saturday or the barbie on Sunday."

"Yes, I can see that . . . but hell it was not," I added severely. "Not in comparison."

"No. Youthful overstatement," he said, turning to look at me, and grinning cheekily. "Anyway, Dad may have ideas about my working my way into favor with the family for all the wrong reasons, but not me."

"You don't give me a very pleasant impression of your father."

"I guess I don't. I guess I *can't*. He's more . . . pathetic than pleasant. I'm his favorite, but he can be a real pain a lot of the time."

"Well, I don't suppose I'll ever meet him, and it's a good thing we two can jog along without any mutual suspicions."

"That's right. I'm not a bludger. I wanted to clear this up, because there's something I want to ask you, and I don't want you to take it the wrong way, get all suspicious."

"Oh?"

"You see, there is something else I'd like to get to see, while I'm staying with you."

I anticipated him, to cover his embarrassment.

"The Bank, of course. You'd like to see the Bank."

He let out a long breath of relief. "You realized? You're very sharp."

"I'm a banker and a politician. One develops a nose for what people want."

"You're right, of course. I would very much like to see the Bank."

"Well, I don't see why that shouldn't be arranged."

CHAPTER SIXTEEN

At the Bank

It was a great pleasure, nearly a week later, to go up to London by train with Ed. We parked the car in the tiny forecourt of the station, and waited for the early train that deigned to stop at so unpretentious a stop on the LMS network. That it stopped at all was probably a relic of Blakemere houseparty days, when on Monday mornings guests without cars would cluster on Melbury station. often with their servants, everyone pleased to escape from the gargantuan excesses of Blakemere to a world more adapted to an ordinary human scale.

"I go first class as a government minister, even such a very junior one," I said to Ed. "You can come with me. We might as well make the most of it while we can. First class will probably be abolished after nationalization."

"I can't see that it makes much difference," said Ed disparagingly, after the train had steamed ponderously in and we had gone through a filthy door into a distinctly tatty carriage.

"It's really just a question of the number of people around you," I said. "Though that's a matter of temperament, of course. I've been used to solitude from childhood, and I've come to like it. And I've always got government papers to go over, which I can't do with people looking over my shoulder."

However, I did very little of going through black boxes on that journey. Fortunately I only had routine meetings in my diary when I got to the Foreign Office later in the day. It was a delight to point out all the places of interest on our short but very slow journey to London. And the first point of interest was the view of Blakemere from the distance.

"Magic!" said Ed, with wonder in his eyes.

"You've no idea how many thousands of cartloads of earth went into the making of that setting," I said dampingly. "There's that character in one of those awful Hemingway novels who keeps asking his woman whether the earth moved for her after they've made love. Well, it certainly moved for my great-grandfather."

"You mean it's not—not *natural*?" Ed asked.

"Very un. Like much of what has gone on there."

Ten minutes later, we saw Tillyards, also in the distant mist.

"That's where Gabriel South, whom you met last week, was brought up," I said. "In the coachman's house, which you can't see from here. His mother was the best friend I ever had, but his father was an unpleasant man."

Ed took the opportunity to shoot at me a question he had obviously been wanting to ask.

"Why didn't you ever get married?"

" 'Nobody asked me, sir, she said.' " That wasn't an honest answer, and I amended it. "Oh, I expect they would have done, if I'd ever shown the slightest interest. For my money, if for nothing else. But I never developed a sense that would have told me when it was my money they were after, or when it was me—and, all things being equal, I assumed it was generally my money. . . . That's a fine Saxon church—one of very few in the country. Are you interested in churches?"

"I'm willing to give them a go. In Australia a nineteenth-century church is considered ancient."

"Nineteenth-century churches could come back into vogue," I said judiciously. "There are some decidedly attractive neo-Gothic ones."

"As opposed to houses, mansions, things like that," said Ed, with a wicked grin.

"Domestic architecture? Never!" I said magisterially, conscious that I might be proved wrong in Ed's lifetime, but certainly not in mine.

"The day war broke out"—one can't say that without thinking of the not very funny comedian on the wireless whose catchphrase it is. But there aren't any convincing other ways of saying it. The day war broke out was a Sunday, and Blakemere was open to the public for the last time that summer. There was no member of the public in the house. Everybody was expecting the announcement that Chamberlain made on the BBC at eleven o'clock (and most people were half expecting the air to be immediately thick with enemy aircraft). I listened in the kitchens with the skeleton staff that was all the house boasted in 1939.

"How incredibly feeble!" I said, as he finished. I was not then a member of the Labour Party, but I quite soon became one.

"But he's done his best, poor man," protested the cook.

"He sounds as if he's taking it as a personal insult," I explained. "He'll never rise to the occasion. Come along: the first thing to do is start shutting the house."

I set them on to draping the furniture in dust sheets. We had collected them in readiness several days before, a whole roomful of them. I myself made a big, and unnecessary, HOUSE CLOSED notice, and drove down to stick it on the gates. Then I went back up to the house and did the rounds of the principal rooms, picking out the pictures and objects which were of artistic value—the early Gainsborough, the Guardi, the School of Van Dyke—with a view to having them collected and put into store. I had got some way with the task when I realized that my secretary, Joyce Oldham, was showing signs of going to pieces, so I set her on to phoning round and sending messages via the postmistress at Melbury to men whom we would need in the next few days to board up the place. Some calls in I noted there was still a note of hysteria in her voice that would give a very bad impression, so I took over myself (she later went entirely to pieces, and I sent her out of the way to the Shetlands, where she married a Norwegian sailor).

By midafternoon there were nearly twenty men up at the house, most of them boarding up the windows, though I commandeered some of them to help me to move some basic items of furniture to the gatehouse, which had been disused for nearly fifteen years. One of the men who helped bring bed, tables, chairs, sideboard, and smaller essentials was Fred Burke, son of one of the Blakemere pensioners I was interested in. He had a small farm now, but he knew me quite well.

"Reckon you're right glad to be moving in here, Miss Sarah," he said, as we surveyed the little living room.

"I am. It's liberation. I should have done it years and years ago. I shall feel like a giant in a house like this, and it'll be a good feeling."

"Was that why you disliked the old house?"

"One of the many reasons. Of course I know that your father was one of the old, faithful servants up there, Fred."

He grinned slowly. "Oh, he never liked the place, miss. Loved the grounds, they were *his* in his estimation, his territory, like, but he never felt comf'table in the house."

"Was there any particular reason for that?"

He looked suddenly down at the floor. "Same as you, I expect, miss. Made him feel small."

"Your father enjoyed a very generous pension from the Fearing family."

"Oh, my father was very grateful for that. He'd worked here since the house was barely begun, moved a lot of the earth for the site, and he was grateful for all the consideration shown, and the good wage." He looked at me meaningfully. "My father would do anything for the Fearings, Miss Sarah."

"Fred, what *exactly* do you mean by that?"

"Oh, just generally, Miss Sarah. Like he felt grateful for a lifetime of work."

We were interrupted by a ring on the telephone I'd had installed in the gatehouse earlier that week. There had been an air raid alert over London. When I finished the call, Fred had taken himself off. Once upon a time, a local who was talking to a Fearing would wait until he was dismissed by a word or a nod. Times had changed. I had helped to change them, and I was glad.

I had no fears that the Führer had put Blakemere at the top of his list of war targets. He was not that discriminating. I extinguished all the lights, and in the gathering dark I walked toward my old home. The boarding-up had only just started, and would take days yet, but a significant number of windows around the Grand Entrance had plywood panels nailed over them, giving them a painful, blinded appearance. The house was closed down, just as the country was cut off.

You won't be opened up for a while, I thought. Then I amended that: *I have just had you closed down for good.*

When we got to Marylebone we took the Underground to the Bank. Ed was obviously surprised: he must have expected I would be met by an official car—either one from the Foreign Office, or one from Fearing's.

"We don't do things that way anymore," I said, speaking for both institutions. "It may come back, but at the moment it's Shanks's pony."

Once down in the bowels of the earth, as he put it, Ed was enchanted with the new experience. He had used buses on his previous trips to London, and I suspected he had been more nervous of going underground than he would have admitted, and was glad of a companion. Once down the escalator he took to it immediately, and felt the speed and convenience of the ride more than he felt the loss of anything to see.

"Mostly it's just tall buildings, and you don't know what they are," he said, with his naive honesty. "With now and then something popping up that you think you should recognize, only you don't."

We got out at Monument, and walked to Lombard Street, with me pointing out a few of the more notable institutions, as well as what had been destroyed on the terrible bombed sites. He had seen plenty of these on previous visits, but found the destruction in the City itself sobering.

"They really had it in for you guys," he said, before he went silent.

Fearing's Bank survived, however, as did Blakemere, proof that the protecting gods were blind. The Bank is a dirty, heavy, but confidence-inducing block of stone from the 1840's, but once inside the working habits have changed a great deal from the Dickensian-style counting house it must have been then. Many of the modern practices were brought in by me. I was greeted with great respect by newer employees, mostly returned from the war, and with respectful friendliness by the older ones. Ed was quiet and watchful, eager to know how things were done, anxious to catch the tone. I took him straight to Digby's office—my old one, on the third floor—and introduced the pair to each other.

"Our Australian relative," I said ambiguously. "Do you have anyone spare who could show him round, tell him what we do, for an hour or so?"

A young man was found, someone who has been invalided out of the forces after D day, and was sufficiently up in the Firm's affairs by now to make a good guide of around Ed's age. I sat in the seat of the suppliant customer or client. Digby could never persuade me to resume my old seat, which was now, and maybe would be forever, his. Fearing's Bank, like Blakemere, was part of my past.

"Seems a nice enough lad," he said in his dry, cool way.

"Seems so," I agreed. "Can't say I really know him yet."

"And . . . what are his plans?"

"You mean what is his interest in the Bank?"

He gestured that I guessed right.

"Can't say I know that yet, either. And I don't know what I'd do if he did show an interest. . . . I do realize that you and your children are concerned in the whole business of what happens to the Bank, Digby."

He shifted in his seat. "I rely on your fairness, Sarah. It's something I've never doubted. You've always been completely open, and completely even-handed. Being your deputy here has been one of the great satisfactions of my life, and I hope I haven't been a disappointment."

"You haven't."

"Anything else is a bonus. Unlike you I'm a natural conservative, small and large c, and I'd like to see the Bank remain in family hands. Beyond that, I know that it's all up to you."

"You're too good for this world," I commented drily.

He smiled his tiny smile. "Are you quite sure who this lad is now?" he asked. He was a man who liked his world ordered, his facts certainties.

"Not quite. In fact not at all. He says he's the grandson of Frank Fearing."

Digby betrayed no emotion.

"That fits in, doesn't it? Or at least it's perfectly possible. I never heard that anyone knew anything about him, other than that he went to Australia."

I watched Digby's face as I brought my suspicions out into the open with him for the first time.

"I have always been of the opinion that he never left Blakemere. That he died on the night of the big family conference about his marriage."

His was a banker's face. It didn't flabbergast easily. He frowned, but a mere suspicion of a frown.

"Have you any reason to think that?"

"Yes," I said shortly. "Did no rumors of the kind ever come to you? From your father, for instance? He was there."

"Nothing at all. He was a wily old bird. He could keep his counsel. Especially if it was made worth his while."

"It would have been. His later years were more prosperous than his earlier ones, weren't they?"

"Oh, yes. That was because of work he was doing for the Bank, he always said."

"Hmmm. Could be true. But then *that* could have been part of the bribe. Of course Aunt Clare's son Leopold could have changed his name when he went to Australia. He had the sort of career where name changes might be advisable from time to time. And Frank was a family name."

He considered this. "Would he have changed it to the name of someone who was presumed himself to have gone to Australia?"

"He might. The name Fearing would have given more confidence than his own, and Frank was one of the senior branch. Perhaps he *wanted* to create confusion, and profit by it."

"What do we know about this boy Ed's grandfather?"

"Not much. He died when Ed was about five. A bit of a joker, Ed says, which I suspect would apply to both. Ed just remembers that, and a long, gray beard. But he said that he was married to a much younger, strong-minded lady, who was doing most of the running of what he calls the 'property' by then, and took it over after he died."

"Which would be about . . . 1930?"

"Roughly. That's what I thought."

Digby was good at quick sums.

"That fits in well with your uncle Frank."

"Fits in well enough with either of them."

"Not really. Frank was born in the late 1850's, wasn't he? So by 1930 he'd be seventy-odd—getting tired, and handing the reins over to a more vigorous, younger wife. I remember Cousin Leopold, but not well. I saw him as some kind of rival, due to all the family talk about the Bank and its future. We met at Frank's wedding in 1893, I remember. He was five years older than me. Born around 1879, then. About the same age as you. So in 1930 he would have been around fifty, fifty-one."

"Perfectly possible to have a gray beard at fifty."

"Perfectly. But losing vitality, and apparently so old?"

"Old-*seeming*. This is to a young child, remember. I'd have thought that eminently possible—even natural."

He gave a wry grin. "I consider the fifties the prime of life."

"You would. You're only just past them."

"All I'm saying, Sarah, is that the story fits better if it was your uncle Frank than if it was your cousin Leopold."

But I wasn't willing to acknowledge that. I didn't think he was making sufficient allowance for the child's eye view. Maybe Digby had never really been a child himself.

When our conversation was over, I went looking for Ed. I wanted to show him at least George Gilbert Scott's Grand Staircase in the Foreign Office, then perhaps send him off to the Abbey and Westminster Hall. But he was deep in Bank duties and procedures with his new friend, and was already committed to lunch with him, and to another session in the afternoon. Well, he'd no doubt had his fill of the company of an old woman like me. I shrugged, smiled at the pair of them, and retraced my steps to get a tube train to Westminster and the Foreign Office.

I was caught in the corridor of its first floor by the shambling, wheezing, smoke-puffing figure of Ernie Bevin, the Foreign Secretary. Actually, everyone else calls him Ernie, but I usually call him Bev. Ernie is the name of my dog—called after him. Besides, I had the healthiest respect for him, and liked him, but Ernie sounded too friendly for someone I suspected I would before long have big rows with, probably over Palestine. But we had a very genial joshing sort of relationship. I was not on that terrible, intimidating list of people he despised.

"Hello, Sal. Up for a few hours' work?"

"My token appearance of the week," I agreed.

"Then back to the stately 'ome," he wheezed on. "Some people do 'ave it good."

"I should think my gatehouse is considerably smaller than your home," I said. "And most of its furniture is on its last legs."

"So you always say. I bet it's grand beyond my imagining. I see we've got something fascinating lined up for you this afternoon," he went on, with relish. "A delegation of Foreign Office dowagers! They'll give you a hot 'alf hour!"

"I'm prepared for them," I said confidently. "They won't get far with me. I do seem to get all the rotten jobs."

"You probably think it's because you're a woman, don't you?" he said, puffing a rich-smelling smoke into my face. "Well, it's not. It's because you're the most junior thing around here. Only an MP for two years, only properly elected a year ago, and straight into the government. Not a top job, hadmittedly, but nobody in their senses would sneer at being Hunder-secretary of State at the Foreign Office. Landed on your feet in politics, didn't you? Of course you get all the rotten jobs."

"I'm not complaining," I said. "I've had the most interesting year of my life—better even than Nazi code-breaking. I don't expect this to be the most fascinating meeting of my time here, but I've seen enough of ambassadorial and consular widows to have a good idea what I'm in for."

I was wrong. I couldn't remotely have guessed what I was in for."

CHAPTER SEVENTEEN

Diplomatic Wife

The delegation was due at half past two, and was ushered in by the minorest of civil servants (a man with a staggeringly brilliant Oxford First in Hebrew), who gave them more deference than I would have been inclined to. Probably it was his way of preparing them for inevitable disappointment. The more sensible of the diplomatic relicts wore dark, simple dresses, with no more than a piece of token jewelry. One had even gone so far as to choose a shabby dress. Most, however, could not resist old habits: for a visit to the Foreign Office one decked oneself out, made oneself up, had hair permed, all in the name of "keeping up standards" (a phrase I expected to hear more than once during the deputation's stay). So there were satin and silk and crêpe-de-chine, there were ropes of pearls, dangling diamond earrings, ruby rings on gnarled, beveined fingers. Anyone could have told these ladies this was foolish policy, probably they knew it themselves, but they were visiting the new Labour Party masters of their old stamping ground, and they were anxious to assert, now Attila the Hun was in control, that they had been part of an older, more gracious, more refined régime. Perhaps that was why I had been chosen to receive them: they would all be aware that I could buy them up, rings, pearls, and all, and not notice any depreciation in my bank balance.

Or perhaps they gave me the job in the hope that that thought would sober them up, moderate their militancy. If so, they were mistaken.

It was a delegation of about a dozen, and they sat around in my large, elegant office, gracefully positioning one leg over the other, exposing silk stockings and high-heeled shoes, their elderly-vulture faces covered in whatever they had acquired in the way of foundation cream, powder, and lipstick, to lessen (without hiding) the ravages of time. This was the more foolish, and larger section of my delegation. They were also the less pleasant: they had a grievance, and the grievance was that their pensions as diplomatic widows had last been raised in 1937, and they were now (they said) seriously embarrassed by its inadequacy.

"We have represented our Country abroad, our Husbands were directly appointed by the King," said their leader, Lady Greystone, who could speak capital letters like no one's business, "and it is natural that people should continue to see us as Representatives, should see our treatment by The Country as a yardstick of The Country's respect and gratitude for all We, and Our Husbands, have done in the past."

"It's a question of keeping up standards," said a second voice. It was a lady of seventy-plus, in a pale orange silk blouse, smartly cut tan skirt, and pearls you could hang a man with. I nodded casually to register the remark, and looked elsewhere for follow-ups.

There were a great many of these. The country would be judged, we the Labour government would be judged, by the way we treated the widows of their diplomatic representatives abroad. The argument was too absurd to be listened to. We would be judged on how we got the country back to work and on how we brought equality and fairness into its social system. My mind strayed. Something had caught my eye about that second voice in the orange silk blouse: the shape of her face, the tilt of the head. She was not the leader of the delegation, but she was an enthusiastic backer-up.

"When my husband was in St. Petersburg," she was saying, "long before it was Leningrad, *of course*, long before anyone had heard of such a *per*son as Lenin . . ."

I put on an expression of great interest, as if doings in Tsarist Russia could tell us a great deal about how affairs should be conducted in the world today. But when the baton had been passed on in the talk-relay and it was safe to do so, I cast my eye down the career details supplied to me by our bureaucrats, details covering all the ladies in the delegation.

This looked like her. Lady Talbot-Boothe. Hadn't I seen that name somewhere before? The final "e" rather set it apart. Husband had been some kind of undersecretary in St. Petersburg in the nineties. Very undistinguished career, climaxing in Consul in Cracow in the early thirties, and Ambassador to Yugoslavia briefly in 1934–5. Typical of the Foreign Office to appoint a nincompoop to a sensitive area like Yugoslavia, no doubt through some collective scorn for the Balkans generally. They had learned nothing from the events of summer 1914. Indeed, the more I saw of Foreign Office civil servants, all recruited from the brightest Oxbridge had to offer, the more I thought them incapable of learning from any experience whatsoever.

I looked at Lady Talbot-Boothe again. The heavy makeup had to contend with the fact that the face was collapsed, had bags in places that had once been firm and china-doll-like. When she nodded vigorously, the bags seemed to take on an independent life of their own, wobbling in all directions. Evelyn, Lady Talbot-Boothe. The Christian name meant nothing to me, but somewhere or other I had encountered the surname.

It was time to make some response.

"Of course I shall take all you have said to me very seriously, and talk the matter over with the Foreign Secretary. You must realize that the government is having similar representations made to us on behalf of many groups—to take an obvious example, the widows of men killed in the war." (Common soldiers' widows! their expressions said. You are comparing us with common soldiers' widows?) "This is a time for tightening our belts. All over Europe people are starving, in the aftermath of war." I refrained from mentioning the Germans—everyone except the occasional clergyman was outraged at any mention of their pitiable state. "Our friends the French are suffering appalling hardships. In any case, as experienced Foreign Office hands, you won't expect a reply from me today. I can only assure you again that . . ."

And so on. As I talked—and talking in this vein was becoming second nature to me, though it made banking talk seem direct and to the point—I could keep my eye on Lady Talbot-Boothe. She had, throughout the meeting, looked approving and interested at each speaker, like a lady used to running committees, used to pretending that what was being said was of great interest to her. But I had got the idea that as she looked from one person to the next, she always shot a glance at me—was really more interested in me than in any other person in the room. Now she was concentrating her attention on me I had an additional impression: that behind the false display of interest and attention there was a glint of malevolence in her eye. As if she had some grudge against me or my family, or maybe some congenital dislike of what we represented. It was disconcerting, but I did not allow myself to falter in my platitudes. I prided myself on being the complete professional. Being in banking had been a schooling in imperturbability.

When I had finished there was really little more that they could say. It was what they had steeled themselves to expect from a Labour minister.

"*So* kind of you to give us of your time," cooed Lady Greystone insincerely. "I'm sure that in the discussions you will do the best you can for us."

The pushing back of seats, the taking leave and saying farewell, were all done in a socially approved, embassy-established way. Some came up and had a "special word" or shook my hand. None said that it was a special pleasure to find a woman in a post of responsibility at the Foreign Office. I can only assume none felt it.

I was watching for Lady Talbot-Boothe, and she, I sensed, was watching for me. She was having a side conversation, seemed to be unduly prolonging it, and when her interlocutor dragged herself away, she turned and came over to thank me for my time—as if I had any choice but to give it. By then she was one of only two or three left in the room.

"*So* kind of you—and such a thrill for all of us to be back in the old place," she said. She paused. It was an opening for me, and intended as such.

"I have a feeling we ought to know each other," I said, with a tentative smile. "But I can't see we can have met at anywhere where your husband was posted."

She gave a knowing yet secretive smile.

"Oh, no. I'm sure you never met *him*. I'm not even sure that we have ever met. Perhaps when you were a young girl. But"—and here the malicious glint came unmistakably into her eye—"your family has been very generous to me over the years."

That was it! The list of my family's pensioners. The name had been on it, without my querying who it was or why it was there. It had been one of several names that rang no bells.

"Ah! Of course many of the people who—" I tried to put the matter tactfully—"to whom we regarded ourselves as being indebted were people I never knew myself. You say we could have met when I was a little girl?"

"I would have been not much older myself." She seemed to say this not only from a misplaced concern about her age, but in order to play with me further. "I think what you recognized was a family resemblance. I and my sisters were always considered very much alike by people in the neighborhood."

"You and your sisters?" I said, with ominous presentiment.

"I was Mary Coverdale's sister. I was the eldest: *Miss* Coverdale, as I was always called—one of those old usages that seems to have faded, more's the pity."

"I see." We shook hands again, rather awkwardly. I had an odd sense of handling this encounter badly, of already being at a disadvantage. "Of course I knew both your sisters, though the younger one not well. How interesting that we should meet up again like this. You say that my family has been—"

"Very generous." It was not said in a grateful tone. But it was not unusual for recipients of bounty to feel no gratitude. "My father died soon after the beginning of the First War, and my brother was killed in the trenches not long after that. Since then . . ."

"I see. I'm sorry not to be better up in our financial affairs." We were by now, of course, completely alone in the room. "I think there may be a little more coffee in this pot. Would you care for another cup?"

She smiled, a purely social smile, verging on the glacial.

"How kind of you. Good coffee is not easily come by these days, is it?"

But again I was struck by the malice, not just in her eyes, but in the tone of her innocuous remarks. We sat at a side table, I poured two cups, and handed her cream and sugar. She helped herself liberally to both.

"Luxury!" she said. Then drew back. "It must seem to you that I really shouldn't have been with this deputation, being so well provided for by Fearing's Bank."

"I'm sure you're not the only one with other sources of income," I said, placatingly. "You were putting a general case, weren't you?" (Like hell they were putting a general case!)

"True, true," she said, nodding her head vigorously and causing the bags and pouches to go bobbling off on their independent ways. "And it dies with me! The agreement was that it was continued to the next generation, but not beyond. My sister has cancer, and Peter of course is long dead."

"That was sad. I liked and respected him very much."

The eyes sparkled with tiny daggers.

"He needn't have volunteered for active service, you know! He was senior enough to have a desk job, and too old to be on the battlefield—not much short of forty!"

It was said not in terms of admiration but of grievance. His death had virtually seen the end of her family, and the prestige a living family name brought with it. I was confirmed in my belief that Peter was the best of his family.

"I'm sorry. I'm quite sure your brother was very brave, and I rather think he died as he would have wished. So the pension dates back to—when?"

"Eighteen ninety-six. Not the time of the marriage, though your grandfather was very generous at that time."

"Grandpapa . . . could be generous."

"Well, he more or less had to be, didn't he?" Here the venom showed clearly through, and a strong vein of commonness, which spite often brings out. "The marriage would never have taken place if he hadn't been generous."

"I was still in the schoolroom at the time. We heard nothing about arrangements with your family. The talk was that Uncle Frank's debts had all been paid."

"So I heard. I wasn't party to the details, either—my husband and I were in St. Petersburg, a fairy-tale posting, his first. All I know I heard much later, from my father. Of course the family was not at all happy with the proposed match."

"No?" I tried to keep the surprise out of my voice, and the disbelief. That had not been at all my impression at the time. But Lady Talbot-Boothe hardly bothered to hide her contempt.

"Well, hardly. Of course we don't take any notice of that sort of thing these days," (oh *don't* we?) "but rich bankers? I'm afraid, to put it bluntly, you weren't the sort of people the Coverdales were used to marrying into." Personally I thought that the Coverdales had been very willing to swallow their pride and principles at the prospect of *very* rich bankers as in-laws, but I held my peace. "The Coverdale baronetcy dated back to 1624, you know. One of the oldest in the country."

I refrained from saying that baronetcies were bought from the early Stuarts as surely as they were bought in the twenties from Lloyd George. Instead, I said, "Was it your sister Mary, then, who insisted?"

"By no means! At least not at first. She was very far from enthusiastic, though her reasons were primarily . . . personal."

"Personal?"

She looked down, as if talking reluctantly, though I think everything she said and did had a purpose.

"She had had an . . . unfortunate experience in early girlhood. The thought of . . . the intimate side of marriage revolted her."

That, at least, was news to me, though it didn't altogether surprise me. But it could not be said to slot anything else into place.

"I see," I said slowly. "That sort of experience is more common than people like to acknowledge."

"I wouldn't know. But Mary would certainly have preferred to stay unmarried. Your uncle gradually realized this."

"I'm afraid I'm still not understanding this," I said, more briskly. "They *were* married. The marriage produced Richard, poor boy."

She smiled, chillingly.

"You perhaps were not aware of your uncle's taste in women?"

That nonplussed me.

"I . . . well, no. I never met any of Uncle Frank's women friends. I heard talk—I *over*heard talk, to be absolutely frank—about his having illegitimate children."

"Quite. But you heard no talk about the mothers?"

"No. I've never known anything about them. I assumed they were paid off."

"Oh, they were. The Fearings are good at paying off people, aren't they? The point was (I'm *told*—of course I knew nothing of the women personally) that the mothers were very young. Thirteen in one case, fourteen in another. It was whispered that his taste ran exclusively to very young girls of a . . . let's say working-class background. Rural or metropolitan, I believe. There was talk, my husband told me, at the Travellers Club of girls in Whitechapel and suchlike areas of London."

"But . . . but . . . I can see why Uncle Frank had to pick someone very different from the sort of girl he preferred, but I still can't see why the marriage took place at all, if your sister was so hostile to the idea of matrimony."

Lady Talbot-Boothe was silent for a moment.

"I was not there, you understand. . . . I think the marriage was in the nature of a bargain."

"And what Uncle Frank offered your sister Mary was—?"

"The future as hostess of Blakemere."

That certainly squared with what I had overheard and what I had felt by intuition at the time. Mary had not been at all as contemptuous as her sister had imagined of the meretricious appurtenances of a rich banking family, and nor for that matter had her father. I remembered my sight of him in the gallery, costing our pictures.

"I certainly had the impression while your sister was living at

Blakemere," I said carefully, "that she was carving a niche for herself as the future mistress of the house."

"Mary was a vigorous, enterprising person. She enjoyed exercising power, being responsible for people, places, for things going well. A type not unlike yourself, perhaps."

I swallowed, but did not rise to the bait. "Go on."

"She had great drive, ambition, organizing ability—she could galvanize people to work for her. She would have made a wonderful chatelaine for Blakemere."

More likely she'd have galvanized half of Buckinghamshire into a peasants' revolt, I thought grimly. And this power house apparently spent most of her days as companion to an elderly relative. I felt great pity for the relative in question.

"What chance would she have had of exercising all those gifts as a spinster, as things were then?"

"Precious little," I agreed. "You had to make your own chances, as a woman."

"She did, or tried to. She swallowed her pride, and her distaste, and . . . came to an understanding with your uncle."

"I see," I said, but getting only a glimmer. "And that was—?"

"That she would marry him, but once an offspring had been conceived it would be a marriage in name only, and . . . relations would only be resumed if the offspring turned out to be female. Once a male heir was born they would cease for good."

I wrinkled my nose in distaste. It added a new layer of sordidness to an already self-interested marriage. My informant did not seem to share my distaste—accepted it as a matter of course.

"It suited them both," said the onetime Miss Coverdale. "Your uncle was explicitly empowered to follow his own interests as long as the marriage lasted."

I took her up on one of her words. "Explicitly? Do you mean this was all in *writing*?"

"Oh, yes. They went in secret to a lawyer and had a formal document drawn up. How far it would have had any legal validity I don't know, but Mary would only marry on those terms."

"It sounds so . . . so unlike my uncle Frank."

"Did you really know him? Can a child ever *know* anyone with the passions and cares of an adult?"

It was a fair point, though pretentiously put.

"I'm beginning to think not."

"It was an excellent bargain from his point of view. Apart from getting his debts paid by the family, he got a marriage in which he was virtually free to do whatever he wanted. And he had provided an excellent hostess for Blakemere."

That set me thinking. If I did not understand my uncle Frank, I at least *knew* him, which this unpleasant woman probably never had. Distasteful as I found the arrangement, and despite the poor light in which it cast my beloved uncle, I seemed to detect in it a glint of his characteristic humor. Frank wouldn't have cared a fig about providing Blakemere with a hostess. But I wondered whether, forced to marry by the pressures of his family, he hadn't got his own back by providing them with the sort of woman who would use her position to boss and blackmail them when it suited her, or ignore them when that was her whim. He—the most cosmopolitan and sophisticated of the family—would have recognized that it would have been a takeover of the vulgar Fearings and their ostentatious home by the gentry—and by one of the gentry who possessed all their worst qualities at their sharpest: their snobbery, their ludicrous pride of birth, their rudeness, their arrogance. His parents would have hated her, his brother, too, all Blakemere's army of staff. It was a clever piece of revenge.

"I think I'm beginning to understand."

"I'm surprised you don't know more yourself," she said, the glint back in her malicious, baggy eyes.

"Nobody told me," I said simply.

"Well, of course it all had to be kept secret, but I would have thought that *you* . . . Anyway, as you know, the marriage went ahead, after my father had laid down stiff financial terms, which meant a good settlement on Mary for life. You were at the wedding, I believe, and by the time they came back from their honeymoon Mary was in the family way."

"I remember Uncle Frank looking so . . . jaunty."

"It was because the bargain was fulfilled, and he was now free to pursue his real interests," she said sourly. "He was a complete degenerate, your uncle."

" 'Judge not, that ye be not judged,' " I said.

The reply came back with the speed of a pistol shot.

"I have no fear of being judged on *that* sort of score, I assure you!"

The mouth set in a firm, self-righteous line, but a fleshy pouch wobbled beside it, the sunken remnant of a blooming cheek. I waited. She would tell me what I wanted to know. She herself wanted so much to tell it. My ignorance acted as a stimulant, an aphrodisiac. "The pregnancy apparently went well. Mary never was told there was cause for disquiet. I believe the best medical man was called in."

"Possibly. The most expensive is not necessarily the best."

"Quite!" She seized on this as more evidence of my family's vulgar ostentation. I was perfectly happy to admit it. "My sister was in her element those months, I'm told. She was not obliged to have a great deal to do with your family, and she began to get her own people around her . . . people who were pleased to have a good old *local* family established at Blakemere. It would have given . . . legitimacy to the place. When it came, the labor was long and hard—"

"I remember it," I said. "I think it was then I decided I would never go through that myself."

"—but the result was satisfactory, at least to all appearances. Things fell apart as soon as it was realized Richard was an idiot."

"I would rather you did not use that word," I said in a hard voice.

"Retarded," she said, with a contemptuous wave of the hand. "I'm afraid I don't come from a squeamish generation. I call things by their names. Mary blamed the doctors, of course."

"She may have been right, though I never saw any evidence."

"She was determined to have the next one in London, where she could be *sure* of the best attention. She wanted the boy put away in an institution. But what she wanted above all was another heir to Blakemere. She was by now determined to be its hostess. And there was no reason to think a second child would be anything other than normal and healthy."

"And my uncle Frank refused to . . . resume relations."

"Absolutely. I think maybe Mary didn't play her cards well. She couldn't hide her distaste for the boy Richard. She had always hated things that were in any way damaged, imperfect. We mustn't blame her. It must be terrible for a woman to go through all the horrors of pregnancy and then produce . . . something like *that*."

I left a tingling silence.

"Anyway, your uncle insisted that he had fulfilled to the letter the agreement they had made. And in point of fact he had."

"The agreement, I suppose, specified 'male child'?"

"Yes! Mary had no reason to foresee the awful thing that actually happened. There was no strain of idiotism in our family." (Or maybe it had spread itself thinly, I thought.) "So she had to find other ways of . . . persuading her husband. It was a difficult situation, because neither of them *enjoyed* what needed to be done, if you catch my meaning."

"Oh, I catch your meaning. It was ironic in a way—almost a punishment for the sordid agreement they had made. But I suppose the situation was not unknown in old families needing an heir. It was a duty rather than a pleasure. I always thought your sister was rather lacking in—let's call it human understanding."

She pursed her lips and fluttered a painted eyelid. "Maybe. She had a fine, vigorous will. People like that sometimes fail to see other points of view. She chose to . . . arouse his spirit, as she described it to my other sister, by emphasizing Richard's state. She thought that would show him how inconceivable it was that he could be considered heir to Blakemere."

"I'm afraid she misunderstood him entirely," I remarked. "Uncle Frank couldn't have cared a fig for Blakemere, or for whether it had an heir. Or for that matter whether it had a hostess."

"Possibly. I suppose as things turned out you must be right. Anyway, whether it was as a result of Mary's taunts, Frank Fearing apparently conceived a great love for the boy."

"He always had it, right from birth," I said. "The discovery of the brain damage didn't change anything."

"It seems to me, I'm afraid, to verge on the morbid," she said, with the total self-approval of the very stupid. "But, however it was, Mary got nowhere, and was forced to agree to the calling of a family conference."

I nodded. "That I remember, too. That was also unwise. I'm afraid my family understood Uncle Frank no better than your sister did—and they'd had every opportunity to get to know him. The last thing to get him to change his mind was a gathering of relatives to put pressure on him."

"He seems to have been very lacking in right feeling and proper respect, especially for his parents. Of course I know more about the family gathering because my parents were there. Papa told me he was obdurate right from the start; sarcastic, rude, and utterly unreasonable."

"I overheard a little of it," I said. "There was a lot of unpleasantness on both sides. I suspect family conferences are usually like that."

"Perhaps. This became very acrimonious. I'm afraid at the climax Mary did something that . . . that I suspect she may have done often enough when with *us*, at home with the family, that is, but . . . probably she had never done it in front of her husband before."

"What was that?"

"She . . . imitated the look of little Richard—the face, the open mouth, the vacant eyes."

She saw my look.

"I'm not defending her—it was in the worst taste."

"It was disgusting—for his own mother to do that," I said passionately.

"Well, we won't quarrel about that. It pushed your uncle over the top. I'm afraid he was quite insane with hatred. He grabbed a fruit knife from the table and plunged it into her."

"He *what?*"

"She died instantly. We've always been glad of that."

"But—but—"

"You didn't know? You mean you didn't know she died? I've often wondered how much you were told, thought maybe you didn't know *how* she died. But—" Her pleasure at doing the telling was horrible to see.

I turned away.

"But that's quite impossible," I said at last. "I remember my father receiving a letter from her."

She almost laughed. "I assure you he could not have. The dead are sometimes said by credulous people to appear to them on earth, but I've never heard a claim from anyone that they've had a letter from the Other Side. Was your father, perhaps, putting you off the scent?"

"Why should he do that?"

"Your father was himself involved in covering up the murder, you know. And you were always very fond of your uncle Frank, weren't you? I've heard that you were very much neglected by your parents. Could he, perhaps, have wanted to preserve your faith in Frank Fearing, partly out of concern for you, partly from a guilty feeling that your uncle had been a better father to you than he ever had."

I thought that over, cradling my cold coffee.

"I suppose it's possible."

"In any case, the fiction had to be preserved at all costs. The Fearings could not be in any way involved with murder. The stability of the Bank, almost of the Country (or so your family would have liked to think) was at stake. They had to concoct a story and stick to it. We were no more happy to have scandal attached to our name than your family was. When both families realized she was dead, they had to sit round and think up what would make the best story. My father said it was a nightmare."

"And the story they concocted was that the marriage had broken down, Frank had gone to Australia, and Mary had gone back to her family?"

"That would have been in everyone's eyes the likely outcome if your uncle hadn't . . . The first part of it, of course, was true: Frank Fearing went to London that night, and within days he was on a boat to Australia. There was some kind of final pay-off, so he would not arrive there destitute. My parents went home, and the next day they were 'called unexpectedly' to London. News was fed back to Tillyards that Mary had joined them in London, her marriage at an end, then that she had gone to stay with an elderly and sick relative on the Scottish Borders."

"Didn't anybody wonder? Anybody who knew her well? Your sister was an unlikely sick nurse."

"Everybody thought she was ashamed. The failure of a marriage was a cause for shame then. And in addition, the wreck of all her hopes. . . . Mary had made no secret of them, to those close to her. It was thought she couldn't face people."

"In fact, she was buried in the little copse on the far edge of the Blakemere estate."

"I don't know the details. That was taken care of by your papa. All my family knew was that she had been buried, in secret, and that the helpers had been sworn to secrecy and paid handsomely. My father said the how and where of the disposal were immaterial to him. He and my mother had to cope with the appalling shock of a beloved daughter's sudden death, in terrible circumstances, and before their very eyes. I think they behaved very well."

Admirably in character, anyway: they'd pocketed a large lump sum and a subsidy for life and beyond.

"When did you learn all this?" I asked.

"My father told me in the last weeks of his life. The First War had begun, so Peter's life was uncertain. In any case, he had never married. My father had begun to treat me as the future head of the family. In fact it will die out with me. I suppose the same will be true of yours."

"There are more distant Fearings," I said, getting up because I did not want to enlarge on the subject to her. "I really am most grateful to you. It's been an odd conversation, hasn't it?"

"*Very* odd," she said, licking her painted lips with relish. "I find it strange that no one had confided the matter to you before."

"The answer may partly be that as long as my uncle Frank was alive he was liable for prosecution for murder, and my father for a lesser offense. My father died first, so he never broached the matter to me. Also," I added, with an attempt at dignity, "I was an unloved child, as you have hinted. My father and I became quite close by the end of his life, but there was always between us a certain reserve, a sense of areas of the past that we did not care to go into. In business matters we were close, but in personal matters we were . . . reticent.

Well, I think I've taken up enough of your time with my family affairs." That seemed ungracious, so I added, truthfully: "It's been a revelation. Thank you."

She shook my hand, mischief and satisfaction mingling in her eyes. She was very pleased to have rearranged my mental landscape for me. Then she walked out of the room, straight-backed, not quite certain on her feet, but looking for all the world as she must have looked when putting an end to a King's Birthday Party in a foreign embassy, after mixing with dubious emigrés caught in a part of the world they despised.

Leaving me to my thoughts. Except that I had little time to indulge them. I was due to collect Ed from Fearing's at half past four, when we would both head back to Blakemere. One of the flunkies summoned me a taxi, and I walked down the grand staircase I had wanted to show off to Ed, and out into the street. Ernie Bevin was being maneuvered into one of the Foreign Office's official cars.

"Have a hinteresting talk with the old biddies?" he called.

"Very interesting with one of them," I said, bending down to talk through the open window. "I'll tell you about it one day when you've got a couple of hours to spare. But I won't be recommending any extra loot for them."

"That's as well, because we'd hignore it if you did," he said, chuckling with pleasure at putting a top banker in her place. "We're not throwing money around on superhannuated figure'eads."

As he drove off, I settled myself into my taxi. There was an unexploded bomb alert in the Strand, the driver explained, and we'd have to go to the City via Victoria. It suited me. I had some shifting of psychological furniture to undertake.

The first thing I had to face was the change in my mental picture of my beloved, charming, ever-fascinating uncle Frank. He was not as I had always seen him to be. He had entered into a really sordid marriage arrangement, and he'd then climaxed that by becoming a wife-killer. The marriage arrangement I could cope with: I had already taken on board the essential nature of the reluctant union. It had diminished my uncle in my eyes, but I had also regarded it with indignation, as something forced on him by his family. The murder was something else. I told myself to think of it as manslaughter, an act of generous rage at the ridicule of his son. I rearranged my ideas of him around that explanation, to try to see if they fitted.

They *nearly* did, but the more I thought about it the more the explanation seemed like special pleading. In fact, it would make more sense to see my uncle as a charming figure but a totally self-indulgent one: someone whose whole life consisted of doing what he wanted, and expecting other people to pick up the bills. Had anything of any geographical or scientific value ever been discovered during those expeditions of his that had cost so dear? Another thought suddenly occurred to me: had he, indeed, ever been on them at all? Were they, perhaps, a cover for months spent around the fleshpots of Shanghai, Cairo, or wherever?

And when Uncle Frank had been forced into actually doing something against his will to get his bills paid (there was, to my banker's brain, something pretty undignified about a man of thirty-odd running up debts and expecting his family automatically to stump up for them), he had made the worst of things by entering into a detailed bargain of self-interest with someone he disliked and despised. He may even have chosen his wife on the basis of preferring someone who would wreak most damage on the Fearing family's self-esteem. When the whole bargain had gone disastrously wrong he had—again, in one of those acts of unchecked impulse and self-indulgence—killed her.

And then there was his relationship with me. Could that have been something very different from what I had seen it as at the time? I faced this possibility with reluctance. It was the most painful thing of all. There had never seemed to me, not then nor since, the slightest cloud of anything—how was one to put it?—anything dubious or dirty in his love for me, in our mutual delight in each other. Yet apparently his "favorite form of sinning is with one who's just beginning" as Leporello sings at Sadler's Wells. His preference was for working-class girls, but still . . . could his attitude to me have been entirely untainted by sex, by lust, call it what you will? Could I be entirely happy knowing the sort of girls, still children, whom he must have gone in search of if he really did frequent the fleshpots of Shanghai or Cairo? Could it not be said, viewed at its worst, that I flirted with him, and he with me? The only difference being that my flirtatiousness was untainted with sex, and that his was not.

A sudden stab of resentment flowed through me: why had he not written to me, as he so easily could? Why had he not wanted to reassure me that he was still alive? Of course there were plenty of reasons, including his liability for prosecution, even possibly for hanging. But could one of them be that, by the time, in his negligent way, he had got around to considering it, I was more or less grown up? Of no interest to him anymore?

And then again that preference for working-class girls: if he had felt it, should he not have mastered it, as many sexual proclivities have to be mastered? But he was obviously not the man to do that, or even attempt it. He was an upper-class exploiter of the unprotected, and one of the worst and most blatant kind. And in this as in other exploits of his, the family picked up the bill and bought the silence of the girls and their families.

My uncle Frank was an amoral, self-indulgent, exploitative cad, a typical leisure-class bounder. And my love for him had left me emotionally ruined. But I put that last thought behind me: I had done too much with my life—far more than many emotionally fulfilled people—to worry about emotional damage.

When we finally got to the Bank I sent the flunkey in to fetch Ed. When he finally jumped into the cab, his whole body showed his excitement. He was full of the wonders of his day, and he went on and on about them as we began the ride to Marylebone.

"That foreign business section fascinates me," he said, among much else. "That's going to take off as things return to normal in Europe. That's where the future lies. One of the blokes there was saying that people shouldn't write Germany off. He says the potential there is fantastic . . ."

I let him go on. Eventually he remembered his manners enough to stop talking about the Bank and inquire about my day. I had my approach prepared.

"Oh, much more interesting than I expected," I said. "In the delegation I was receiving there happened to be your grandfather's sister-in-law—sister of his first wife, that is."

Did I imagine it, or was there a flicker of worry in his eyes?

"Didn't know anything about a first wife."

"Oh, she was dead by the time he married your grandmother," I said. I don't think I imagined his relief. Ed's thoughts were becoming, or had always been, a mite dynastic, for all his naive front and puppyish air of careless blundering. "So there's no question of his children being illegitimate."

"That's a relief," he said, more casually. "Australians are always calling people bastards, but it's better not to be one."

"You mentioned a photograph of your grandfather's wedding day," I went on.

"That's right. On the sideboard back home."

"Was his bride *much* younger than himself?"

"Hell, yes. Hardly more than a girl. These days I reckon he'd get called a cradle-snatcher, or a dirty old man. If you can believe my dad, he had to be forced to actually marry her—a real shotgun affair. With her family holding the shotgun."

"Yes, I don't think my uncle was a man of conscience," I said sadly.

I put the subject aside as distasteful, and let Ed get back to talking about banking. He was still so much of a boy that I was loath to distrust him. Who but a boy would tell me things I was bound to know about every department in a bank I owned and had run? Who but a boy would lay down the law about things I inevitably knew a hundred times more about than he did? There was a delicious naiveté about him that was delightful.

"I really fell for the place," he said. "And by the end of the day I felt I was beginning to understand the system. Do you think it's in the blood?"

"Could be. Let's hope you've missed out on some of the other things that could be there, too."

"It set me wondering: maybe that's where my future lies. It's not often that I've found anything so fascinating from the moment I started to go into it. Do you think I should be considering aiming for a job in a bank?"

"Maybe," I said. "It could be arranged. We have excellent relations with Coutts and Barings, and with most of the big outfits. They might be willing to give you a start. It would be better not to think in terms of Fearing's. It might alarm Digby. And the age of nepotism is over."

"That would be beaut," he said.

Again I thought I detected a dying fall, a note of disappointment, in his voice. I felt my mouth setting itself into a firm line. I am too old to be taken in a second time by male charm.